The Couple On Holiday

A completely addictive and gripping psychological thriller with a heart-stopping twist

Mikayla Davids

For my husband

Prologue

I feel content and peaceful. A calm settles over me. I can't imagine that anything bad could ever happen, here on this beautiful island...

This summer, I'm in paradise with my new husband by my side and my life couldn't be more perfect. Light is filtering through the trees as I fling my arms wide and finish my morning yoga routine. It's a ritual I complete every day, stretching my body as the sun rises. I follow this by making a coffee and sipping the hot, sweet liquid as I go for a gentle stroll.

Each morning I vary my walk, taking in the stunning scenery of the private Caribbean island that's my home for the summer. Yesterday, I walked down to one of the beaches and allowed my toes to sink into the soft, inviting sand. I surveyed the clear blue sea and listened to the birds twittering in the treetops. Today, my feet take me in a completely different direction. I walk round the edges of the whitewashed villa that belongs to my family, and along the winding path that leads to the high clifftop on the north side of the island.

I skirt along the edges of the clifftop, every so often daring myself to look at the vast drop below. As I move, the tension in my muscles loosens. I manage to cover a fair distance and I find myself nearing the section of the cliff which gives way to natural steps and leads down to an idyllic lagoon. It was the place me and my husband went to on the second night of our honeymoon, just under a week ago. A smile plays across my lips as I remember our romantic evening together by the sea, under the stars.

Right now, the sky is awash with beautiful deep pinks, purples and oranges. The turquoise sea contrasts beautifully and it's like I'm looking at a painting. There's a slight breeze and I enjoy the feel of the wind rippling in my hair as I watch a small fishing boat bobbing in the water. I sigh deeply, embracing the day.

Straying to the top of the steps, I look down, wondering whether I have time to descend and take a dip in the ocean before my husband wakes up. But the thought goes straight from my mind as I gaze down the steep, stony staircase and see a red trail of blood.

I freeze, panicked by the sight. It's not just a few blood spots, there's a lot of dark, red blood.

Perhaps an animal has been hurt? Or maybe someone is in trouble?

I take a deep breath, not really wanting to look again but knowing I'd never forgive myself for turning away if I could help in some way.

I stand on the first step and look down at the dizzying drop below. My nails are digging hard into the palms of my hands. I can't see anything, so I take another step, and then another until I'm part way down the twisting route to the lagoon.

And then I see it.

I see the body, crumpled at the foot of the steps. The neck at an unnatural angle.

No-one could survive a fall like that.

I turn around, wanting to put some distance between me and the dead person, knowing I need to report what I've seen straight away.

Instead, I'm jolted by the figure now standing on the top step looking down at me.

My heart hammers in my chest and I fight to keep my balance and stay upright.

Am I next?

Chapter One
Sienna
One week before

'Here we are,' I smile up at my husband. 'Back where it all began.' I grasp his hand in mine. This is the first day of our honeymoon, and the first day of the rest of our lives. We've decided to spend our vacation in the same location where we fell in love – a gorgeous island in the Caribbean. My heart bursts with happiness as I imagine the sun-drenched days ahead of us.

My husband, Owen, picks me up and spins me around. I squeal delightedly, feeling giddy with excitement as our boat pulls up to the jetty.

'Put me down!' I laugh and he obliges.

I take in the familiar curve of the bay, the scenery that's imprinted so strongly in my memories. This to-die-for island just happens to be privately owned by my father. I spent many childhood holidays here with my mother and, in my adult years, it became my haven and my sanctuary. I know I'm beyond lucky as it's the kind of destination most people can only dream of visiting, let alone owning. But, then again, with a family like mine, and the drama and stress that comes with being the only daughter and heiress to the Barker-Jones media empire and fortune, having somewhere like this to escape to is a godsend. During the last few years, I've struggled with the high expectations my parents placed on me. They haven't exactly been supportive of me trying to forge my own way in the world. But I have no desire to follow in my father's footsteps. I hate the way the media has relentlessly invaded every aspect of our family's life and I just want a more normal existence. I've learnt the hard way that money does not buy happiness.

'Here's to our marriage,' Owen whispers in my ear, as he presses himself behind me and wraps his strong arms around my waist. We stand together for a moment, admiring this view of the island. The clifftops towering above us, the long stretch of golden beach complete with palm trees.

'Ready?' I finally say, breaking the spell between us.

'I sure am,' Owen grins, his brown eyes twinkling.

I can't believe that half a year ago we hadn't even met, let alone fallen in love. It feels like Owen has always been a part of my life and yet, in reality, we've only been an item for just under six months. We met by chance, two people from completely different upbringings. But our lives collided here on Oyster Island. At the time, I was going through a particularly intrusive period of media interest as well as hitting my late twenties and feeling like I was totally off track. My love life was in tatters and everything felt as though it was spiraling out of control. So I escaped to my favourite place in the world, just by myself, to recharge and take some time to work out a plan for the future.

Little did I know, I was about to cross paths with Owen Turner. He'd been hired as a new gardener for Oyster Island. He was relatively early on in his career but his talent and hard work had already helped him to forge good contacts. In recent weeks he's mentioned that he'd jumped at the opportunity to work on this private island, despite knowing little about the family who owned it or how different life can be in this small slice of the world. It's definitely breath-taking here, but it can be quite isolating, cut off from everything else. It's easy to pretend to be a modern-day castaway when you're here. And some people struggle with that, even for just a short period of time. Thankfully, this wasn't an issue for Owen.

The boat is secured and a gangplank laid down. I'm the first person off and onto the jetty, eager to officially start our honeymoon and grateful to be able to escape reality for a little while longer.

I think back to the first time we met. I was on one of my regular morning walks when I spotted tall, handsome Owen Turner. He made my heart flip the instant I laid eyes on him. He was working in the grounds of the expansive villa at the centre of the island, the building that is the Barker-Jones residence when we're staying here. The curve of Owen's jawline and the way his muscles moved as he worked, digging in the soil, drew my attention. When he stood up, looking at me directly with a mischievous glimmer in his eyes, and gave me a confident nod, it was love at first sight. I'd never experienced anything like it before.

That's how it all started. I took the plunge and spoke to him. Now, here we are, ready to enjoy paradise together and celebrate our honeymoon. It's funny how life can work out in such unexpected ways.

We step out onto the smooth sand and I sigh with relief. Arriving here always feels like coming home. I'm determined to shake off my worries and just concentrate on making special memories with my new husband. Lacing our hands together, we ascend the steep winding hill that leads to the villa, affectionately called 'the pearl' of Oyster Island by my parents as it is indeed the stunning centrepiece of the island. There's a scattering of other houses, used for entertaining friends or clients, occasionally rented out to celebrities or minor royals who are looking to get away from it all, but none of them are as opulent or impressive as the vast home-from-home that we have for our own use.

'Have you heard from your father?' Owen asks me, immediately shattering my composed surface and splintering my nerves.

'No,' I say, a little more bluntly than I mean to. I unlink my hand from his.

'Sorry,' Owen says apologetically. 'I won't ask if you don't want me to.'

'It's okay... I'm just still feeling a bit emotional about everything.'

My father's reaction to our wedding was not a positive one. Although, to be fair, we did spring the news on him – and after we'd tied the knot as well. I understand he'd felt hurt because he'd always imagined escorting his little girl up the aisle on her wedding day. Things didn't quite work out like that though. Because, after a whirlwind romance, Owen and I got hitched in total secrecy. I knew he was the one for me and I didn't want my parents interfering. So I decided to make our love official before introducing Owen to my family. It was underhand of me, but I didn't want to have to wait for their approval. The heiress marrying the gardener wasn't exactly the marriage match they'd had in mind for their darling daughter but you can't help who you fall in love with. I was determined nothing would come between Owen and I.

'Well, getting married is an emotional time,' Owen says, injecting a light-hearted tone into his words that feels forced and awkward.

'You can say that again,' I quip back.

'Are you sure I haven't messed things up for you?' Owen asks, looking downcast all of a sudden, despite our gorgeous surroundings.

'What? No! Don't ever think that.' I take his hand once more. 'I just hope you don't feel like I've dragged you into my crazy family.'

'Well, you did warn me...'

'True, but there's warning you and experiencing it first-hand.'

Owen had been on the receiving hand of my father's wrath in his first encounter with him. I was mortified that my father had been so openly angry with Owen for not doing the traditional thing of meeting the family and asking permission for my hand in marriage. It's such an old-fashioned attitude but my father is a man who upholds tradition and protocol so I knew the situation would bother him. I just didn't realise to what extent.

I try to brush away the flashback of my father going almost purple in the face as he gave us both a dressing-down, like we were naughty teenagers instead of fully grown adults. I was so embarrassed and wanted the floor to swallow me up. My father had tried to convince us to get an annulment, but I dug my heels in and refused. Nothing could make me give up Owen Turner. He's not like any other man I've ever met. He's a breath of fresh air in my controlled and restricted world. I want my marriage to be a chance for me to reshape my life as well as a new beginning for us both. I'm sure my father will come round soon enough.

We reach the top of the hill, both of us breathing hard from the exertion as we make our way down the pathway and through the gated entrance that leads to the whitewashed villa where we'll be staying.

'You're not as fit as you think you are, Owen,' I joke, shaking away the troubled thoughts connected to my parents' expectations.

'Is that so?' Owen looks at me for a second and then, in a flash, he scoops me up into his arms.

'What are you doing?' I gasp in surprise.

'I'm going to carry you over the threshold, into our new life.' Owen gives me a wink and then marches towards the entrance of my family's villa, still holding on tight to me.

'This is it!' he beams. 'Home for the next few months.'

The door is ajar, the staff have clearly been expecting us, and he barrels us through into the airy hallway. I squirm, ready to be put down, but he doesn't set me on my feet just yet. Instead, he heads for the stairs.

'Where are you going?' I giggle.

'Where do you think?' He winks at me again and my heart flutters in my ribcage. I can't believe I'm married to this handsome man and we're going to have the run of this pretty island in the sun.

In this brief snapshot in time, I feel utterly certain that Owen and I are meant to be. He's exactly what I need: someone normal, to ground me and balance out my complicated family. Because if you scratch the surface of my privileged world, there's a whole web of secrets and lies underneath. Owen came into my life just as I hit rock bottom. Now, with him by my side, the only way is up.

And I can't wait for our married life to properly begin...

Chapter Two
Owen

This doesn't feel real. Only six months ago, I was standing in front of this very mansion, shovel in hand, digging in the soil, my muscles aching and my body sweltering in the heat. I'd lucked out with a job opportunity in the most stunning surroundings I'd ever been to. But, the fact was, I was still working long hours in a physically demanding job. I would never, ever have been able to afford to go somewhere like Oyster Island on vacation myself and the idea of owning even a slice of a place like this was just laughable.

At least it was back then. Everything changed when I met Sienna Barker-Jones. Her golden hair, sky-blue eyes and model looks made me notice her immediately. Although there was something else about her; the tilt of her head and the lost look on her face made me want to find out more. She'd been dressed in yoga pants and a crop top when I first encountered her, so I'd thought she was just another member of staff, going for a morning run before work started. I hadn't been on the island for very long and I was still getting to know everyone.

I had no background knowledge of the Barker-Jones family at that point and I'd never been introduced to any of them, as I'd been hired through their recruitment agency. So I didn't hesitate to strike up a conversation with the stunning blonde. I had no idea that she was the daughter of Derek Barker-Jones, the media billionaire who's known world-wide.

Would that have stopped me talking to Sienna? I may have been less forward, that's for sure, but something made me speak up that day. And I'm glad I did. Because, as mad as it sounds, Sienna is now my wife.

I gaze over at her as she gets ready for our evening meal. She's fixing her gold hoop Tiffany earrings and her hair is swept up, with various plaits intertwining into a bun that sits high on her head. An expensive locket hangs around her neck. I flinch slightly as I think about the combined cost of the earrings and necklace she's wearing. They're both worth more than the monthly wages I used to bring in as a gardener, even surpassing the payment I received when working for the Barker-Joneses. When I was employed to work on the island, my salary was a huge sum of money to me, more than I'd ever earned before, but it's nothing in comparison to the wealth Sienna is used to. I'm only now discovering quite how other level Sienna's world is. This private island with its majestic villa, guesthouses and helicopter landing pad is just a tiny part of her family's property portfolio.

The ring that sits on my wife's slim wedding finger catches the light and sparkles. I bought it for her when we went to the Cayman Islands. It was our pit stop after we decided to leave Oyster Island and before we went on to Cuba for an intimate beach wedding involving just the two of us and the required legal witnesses. I was keen to buy her the most exquisite engagement ring I could afford, and the pear-cut diamond ring is hands down the most expensive thing I've ever purchased. In contrast, it's probably the least expensive bit of jewellery Sienna's worn, but she assured me it didn't matter how much it cost because our relationship means everything to her.

And I believe her.

'Ready?' Sienna asks, catching me admiring her as she turns to find me lying on the bed. I've been patiently waiting for her for the last fifteen minutes, but I don't make any mention of this.

I swing my legs round and pick up my sunglasses from the bedside table. It feels odd not to need car keys or my wallet, but they're buried in the bottom of my suitcase and I won't have use for either of them in the coming few months. Our every whim will be catered for and there's no call for a car here either. There's a couple of those golf-type buggies and a few flatbed trucks for the staff but they're rarely used. It's only a small island, so you can get around it in about an hour on foot. There's not much here, just a few buildings, consisting of the main villa and then a handful of smaller houses used for guests. There's a complex of low-rise, two-storey apartments for the staff, tucked away on one corner of the island. The Barker-Jones family has a number of employees to make sure that everything is kept pristine, from cleaners to pool attendants to maintenance. Every element has been thought about and, as a result, the island retreat is well-tended to and is way more than a five-star experience, it's more like the gold standard.

We make our way down to the dining area, which is at the front of the villa. The room itself is light and airy, with doors that can be thrown open onto a terrace area with incredible views across the east side of the island. Our table has been made up outside, precisely placed to make the most of the view, complete with a pristine white tablecloth.

'Look at that scenery,' Sienna sighs happily.

A waiter is promptly on hand, pouring large glasses of white wine for us both. I recognise him as a guy called Jed. He lived a few apartments along from me and we played cards on a number of occasions to pass the time on hot evenings. I don't know him massively well, but the staff here are a fairly close-knit group. There's usually about twenty-five of them at any one time and they've got their own little community set up in the area of the island designated to them. They have things like their own swap shop, bar and café area set up in a few little wooden huts at the centre of the apartment complex. It always felt like there was a decent vibe amongst the people working here. I only started as a gardener a few weeks before Sienna arrived on her solo vacation, so I didn't spend much time bonding with them all. Although it seems strange to think that I'm not one of them any more.

Sienna leans across the table and kisses me on the lips. The wheel of fortune has finally turned in my favour. I'm quite literally the luckiest guy on the planet. I genuinely care for the woman I married but becoming the husband of someone who will one day inherit an unfathomable fortune has been a massive plus to our relationship. I can't deny that marrying Sienna has been like finding a winning lottery ticket. I worked hard to turn my life around in my early twenties but, given my background, it was an uphill struggle. I was proud of the progress I was making, but the kind of life I have with Sienna now is beyond most people's wildest dreams.

Somehow, meeting and falling and love on this island, the gulf between us didn't seem apparent. We were just two young people who were attracted to each other. We were also two young people isolated on a desert island with not a lot to entertain us, so it's no wonder it was an intense time between us. We had no distractions and only our feelings to focus on.

I take a sip of my red wine and lean back in my chair. The last few months have been quite an eye-opener for me. Travelling from Oyster Island to Cuba on Sienna's private boat, which she'd so lovingly chosen all the interior decor for, was when the penny dropped for me and I realised just how totally different her universe is. Then, after we got married in Cuba, we went to meet her parents in the Victorian residence they have in the heart of Chelsea, in London, where we stayed with them for six weeks. That was the next major wake-up call. Living under the same roof as her irate father and unimpressed mother was not a comfortable experience. I began to wonder if her father was right and we had rushed into marriage too fast. I'd had no clue as to what I'd been letting myself in for when I married into the Barker-Jones family. Sienna was feeling under pressure so she suggested that we come back here to Oyster Island for a while, to take ourselves away from the scrutiny of her parents and enjoy our honeymoon period together.

Getting in the boat, I felt extremely relieved to be returning back to Oyster Island. I thought our differences would just melt away again. Except, now that I'm here, with Jed, my one-time card-playing acquaintance, hovering at my elbow and ready to top up my glass at the nod of my head, things have changed. And we're not going to be able to go back to how things were when Sienna and I were snatching secret moments together and no-one knew we were a couple.

'Madam, sir, we have oysters to start.' With a flourish, Joseph – one of the most senior members of staff on the island – sets down our plates and then discreetly moves away, heading back in the direction of the kitchen.

I stare down at the food before me and my stomach begins to churn. I've never had oysters before and they aren't necessarily high on my bucket list. I'm not big on seafood in general and the idea of eating the slimy contents of the numerous shells makes me want to gag. I guess my aversion to eating fish is something that hasn't come up in conversation between my wife and me before. There's still so much we don't know about each other.

'Did you know that oysters are meant to be one of the most powerful aphrodisiacs?' Sienna says, giving me a coy smile.

'I do... but I don't think we really need any help in that area. Do you?'

Sienna blushes.

Smiling, I say, 'How about we skip the dinner part and carry on where we left off earlier?'

She giggles. 'While that sounds like an appealing idea, I'm starving. All that travelling has made me hungry.' Sienna tucks into her dish and tells me how much she's looking forward to swimming in the freshwater pool again. And how she can't wait to have a long stroll tomorrow morning, to see all of her favourite sights.

I push the oysters around with my fork, reluctant to actually try them. Halfway through her own food, Sienna clocks that I haven't eaten anything.

'Oh, don't you like them?'

I hesitate. I don't want her to know that I've never eaten oysters before. That will just sound completely ridiculous to her, even though the truth is that scampi and chips was the Friday night fish dish that my own family were most familiar with. Just thinking about the greasy paper and smell from the rundown takeaway on the corner of the street where I grew up makes me shudder a little. No wonder fish isn't at the top of the list of my most favourite foods.

'I'm sorry. I'm not big on seafood.'

Sienna gives a little gasp. 'Really? Well that's something we need to change then, isn't it?' She twirls a strand of her honey-coloured hair around a finger – and then goes on to tell me that if we're going to spend our time here in the next few months, I'm going to need to get used to dining on fish, as it's the freshest food that we have access to.

'Go on, just try a bite. You can't come to Oyster Island and not eat oysters. I'm sure you'll change your mind.' Sienna gives me an encouraging smile. I know she means well, but I'm slightly rankled by the suggestion of me needing to change things about myself. I know she probably didn't mean to say it like that, but I'm feeling pretty exposed in terms of my lack of life experience in comparison to the varied lifestyle Sienna has had so this small comment gets to me. Our interactions are usually so in tune with one another, so this exchange feels odd. I know I'm probably overthinking things but this honeymoon – this marriage – is important to me.

I swallow. I should just say no, but I don't want her to think I'm some sort of fussy eater or, worse, someone who isn't going to go out of their comfort zone. I know if this relationship is going to be a success, I'm going to have to compromise and try new things. Sienna is looking so earnestly at me and I remember the oyster shape tattoo she has on her ankle.

'Did you know oysters don't just symbolise love, they symbolise hope and potential as well.' Sienna's face is lit up as she's telling me this. 'And they also represent random chance. You never know which shell is going to contain a beautiful pearl.'

I smile back at her.

'I've always loved the name for this island, but it means even more to me now. You being here was random chance...'

This island means so much to her and what she's just said is so sweet so, without further ado, I kiss her across the table and then I pick up the smooth shell. I tip the fish into my mouth, just as I've observed Sienna doing. It slides down my throat in one swift movement.

'Urgh!' I exclaim. A nauseous sensation rises up in me and I immediately regret my actions. I grab my glass of water and gulp down the liquid.

'Are you okay?' Sienna says, looking both concerned and perplexed.

'Um, yeah,' I stutter. 'Seafood just isn't my thing though... Do you want these?' I push the oysters towards her, eager to get them out of my line of sight.

Sienna shrugs. 'I'll have one or two.'

I have to look away as she digs in. I push down the second wave of nausea that comes over me. I'm trying to control my protesting stomach, but it's no good. The taste of oysters really doesn't agree with me.

'I'll be back in a minute,' I say hurriedly, as I make a dash for the bathroom. Thankfully, I make it there in time and soon I'm feeling much better. Although I'm mortified to have made such an idiot of myself.

I return to the dining room sheepishly. As I do so, Joseph, the ageing butler, passes me and gives me a look of barely concealed contempt. My footsteps falter as he brushes past me in a brash, aloof way. I know I didn't misinterpret the expression on his face but I have no idea why he was staring daggers at me. We've only ever had polite exchanges previously.

Feeling confused, I sit down heavily in my seat.

'Wow, you really don't like seafood then,' Sienna says. 'Do you feel any better?'

'Much,' I say, patting my stomach and gathering myself. 'It was just the taste of the oysters.' I notice our plates have been cleared, so I resolve to sweep away the last half an hour and try to move on. I want to make this the magical evening I know Sienna is hoping for.

Jed is back again, filling up our wine glasses and informing us that dessert will be served soon. He avoids my gaze, his focus completely on Sienna. I wonder if all of the staff are going to behave so awkwardly around me. I suppose I shouldn't have expected anything different.

There are so many challenges from lots of sources around us – her parents, her extended family. Plus the media will no doubt heap all kinds of pressure on us too when the news of our secret wedding eventually breaks. None of that is important though. No-one else really matters, what matters is Sienna. I just want to make her happy. If we can be happy then I've just got to believe that everything else will come good.

But, as the evening progresses, an unsettled feeling begins to grip hold of me and it's nothing to do with the oysters. Being here, in these luxurious surroundings, I wonder if I'm really up to the job of being a husband to someone like Sienna Barker-Jones. I know I'm going to give it my all to try and make our marriage a success.

I just hope my past doesn't ruin my shot at having the perfect life.

Chapter Three
The Killer

Sun, sand and sea. Staff waiting on you hand and foot, Sienna basking in the lap of luxury...

It makes me sick.

Someone like that, spoon-fed the best things in life while treating everyone around her like dirt. It's disgusting.

People like that never truly get their comeuppance. Sure, they might get mean things said about them in the papers from time to time, but real justice? Never.

I'm about to change all that.

Daddy's little princess is going to pay for her crimes, and I'm here to make sure that everything she cherishes here comes crashing down around her.

Because the thing she doesn't realise is that, while in the real world her bodyguards watch her every move and shield her from any threat, here on Oyster Island I can finally get her all alone.

And then I'll get my revenge.

Chapter Four
Sienna

Standing in front of the floor-length mirror, unpinning my honey-coloured hair before I get into bed, I look directly into my own eyes and have a flash of clarity. Owen is important to me for lots of reasons. He's the only person I've ever encountered who genuinely didn't seem to know who I was or have any detailed knowledge of my family when we first met. In that initial conversation we had, I felt like I was talking to someone on an even level for once, with no preconceptions forming a barrier between us. It was so freeing. And, even when he did find out that I wasn't another member of staff, he didn't seem fazed or alter his behaviour as a result.

Despite the craziness of our impromptu marriage and then the interrogation he endured from my father, plus the hostility he received from my mother, he's remained chilled and down to earth. He seems as though he will be loyal and dependable. And, most of all, Owen makes me feel safe. That's vital because in the past I've had to deal with stalkers, death threats and abduction risks. Being the child of someone as wealthy and as outspoken in his views as my father means there's plenty of people out there who harbour a real hatred for the Barker-Jones empire. And, even though I'm now married and offically Sienna Turner, the world will always view me as the only daughter of Derek Barker-Jones.

I change into my satin nightdress and I acknowledge that, as well as making me feel safe in his presence, Owen also seems to enjoy spending time in my company. This is also a novelty, because I don't have many true friends.

You'd think being the daughter of someone so high-profile and wealthy would have gifted me a charmed life and, in lots of ways, it has. My world is gilded with beautiful jewellery, luxurious surroundings and expensive objects. I'm so grateful for all of this. But it does come at a price. My life feels so disconnected with the world. I often feel trapped, in a golden prison, flanked by security and unable to participate in anything beyond the artificial lifestyle my father has crafted for me. I've been isolated in my picture-perfect princess tower, watching out of the window by myself, looking down at everyone around me having fun. Until now. Owen brings laughter to my day.

Turning towards him, stretched out on the bed, I thank my lucky stars our paths crossed and we managed to make it up the aisle together before my father could stop us. I'm now a married woman. This honeymoon is just the start of our lives together. And, as I slide into bed beside my husband, I'm so ready for our happily ever after.

***

I wake up early, at first light. I've always been a naturally early riser. The same cannot be said of Owen. He doesn't sleep super late but he needs an extra hour or so than me. So this is the perfect time in the day to have a little bit of time to myself. I kiss my husband on the forehead and he reacts by sleepily stretching and rolling in the opposite direction.

Dressing quickly in shorts and a loose t-shirt, I tie my hair up in a messy bun and head off towards the kitchen of the main house. I know, even at this early hour, I'll find our housekeeper Molly there, most likely preparing a tasty breakfast treat.

I meander through the high-ceiling corridors, so different to the dark and narrow hallways at my parents' London home. Here I feel like I can breathe properly, move properly, be more myself. The smell of rosemary wafts towards me and my tummy rumbles. I cross my fingers that Molly is making her famous rosemary and olive focaccia bread. It's one of my all-time favourites.

'Morning Molly,' I say breezily, as I wander into the kitchen and find her, as predicted, with her sleeves rolled up and the oven already on.

She turns around and I'm expecting her to give me a quick hug and her usual warm greeting. Molly is far more than a housekeeper to me as she practically raised me. She used to work in my parents' London home and it was Molly, with her kindly smile and rosy cheeks, who would wipe my tears and ask me how my day was when I was growing up. She's in her sixties now, so my parents transferred her and her husband, Joseph, to Oyster Island a few years ago for a change of pace and a slower way of life.

But the hug never comes, instead Molly folds her arms across her ample bosom and looks at me in surprise.

'Molly, it's so good to see you!' I exclaim, stepping forward and opening my own arms to her. Molly doesn't budge though.

'What's wrong?' I ask, with trepidation in my voice. Molly and I have always had such a close relationship. She's been more of a mother to me than my own mother has. And I've certainly spent far more time with her as well.

'What's wrong?' Molly repeats, her Irish lilt still detectable despite her not having lived in the old country for over forty years. 'Can you not guess?'

I'm hoping that her behaviour doesn't have anything to do with Owen. After all, she's told me many times how she and Joseph were once star-crossed lovers. He's a Protestant and she's a Catholic and their romance was forbidden by both of their parents. So they eloped together and set up a new life for themselves in England. They worked in various domestic roles in grand country houses before being employed by my parents as a housekeeper and a butler. They're the most dependable staff we've had and have always been a source of stability for me.

'Owen?' I say his name, although not wanting Molly to confirm my fears.

'Of course Owen,' Molly says, her ruddy cheeks glowing before launching into what's troubling her. 'I can't believe you just ran off with that boy and married him without telling me. Not to mention there being no invite to the big day.'

I flush. It's true that I acted impulsively but I was certain of my feelings and I didn't want anyone, not even Molly, trying to talk me out of it.

'Me and Joseph had no clue,' Molly says, shaking her head disapprovingly. 'You certainly kept it quiet from us.'

'I didn't mean to deceive you,' I start to say.

'Yes, you did.'

Molly has always been forthright in the way she approaches things and so I change tack. 'Okay, I did mean to deceive everyone. But, I thought, you of all people, would understand.'

For once, Molly is lost for words.

'Didn't you always tell me that you and Joseph ran away together?' I wheedle. 'And that when love strikes, you just have to go with it.'

'Oh no,' Molly grumbles. 'Don't tell me that my fanciful stories of first love have made an impression on you.'

Shrugging I say, 'Maybe it gave me a little more courage but, like you always said, I knew the instant I met him. So I acted from the heart.'

All through my early twenties, I tried to engineer different ways to break from living in my parents' shadows. Nothing worked. I had a series of doomed relationships and I wondered if I'd ever find true love in the way Molly and Joseph did. I reached twenty-nine and I'd all but given up. So when I arranged to spend time on my parents' private Caribbean island to reset and work out what to do with my life when I hit thirty, I never expected to meet Owen. He changed everything. I didn't realise how much I wanted this relationship and, now that I've got it, I'm going to do whatever it takes to protect it.

Molly tuts and then finally opens her arms to me. I dash into them and feel her familiar warmth.

After a few moments, I step back to study her properly. 'You're not properly angry with me, are you?' I hadn't been expecting the third-degree from Molly.

'More disgruntled.' Molly stops frowning then and squeezes my hand. 'Because me and Joseph have had no end of questions from your father.'

'Oh...'

'He seems to be holding us personally responsible for you having a summer romance. And he wouldn't believe us when we said we had no idea what was going on under our noses.'

I pull at a strand of my hair. I should've known that my father would want to put the blame at someone's door. He knows what a steadying presence Molly and Joseph have been throughout my life, so I imagine he thought that nothing would get past them while I was staying on the island. I was actually surprised they hadn't cottoned on to the feelings Owen and I had for each other. They're normally sharp about this sort of thing, but then Molly's hair has suddenly got greyer and the lines on her face deeper, and they're both getting a bit older now. Although I know some of the other staff became aware, I guess they must've just thought it was a fling. And I can't see that any of them would have taken gossip to Molly or Joseph. They're fair but they can be stern and I imagine other members of staff didn't want to risk their comfortable jobs by interfering.

'I've never seen him so angry, and that's saying something,' Molly continues. 'Are you sure you know what you're doing with this Owen?'

What she really means is: have I lost my senses?

I sit down on a wooden chair. 'Yes, I promise. I love him.'

Molly seems to accept this and sits down beside me. 'I'm just worried for you, usually you'd come to me with anything like this.'

'I know but... Owen's different.'

'Good different?'

'Good different,' I beam. 'He's the best.'

'Your father's concerned you haven't known him long.'

I shake my head. 'My father's concerned he's only after my money because he doesn't have any of his own.'

'Well, there's that too,' Molly admits.

'It's not an issue,' I say firmly. 'We're married. I'm happy.'

'That's all that matters then. I just pray it works out for you, my love.'

'I've got a good feeling. He's the salt of the earth. Just like you and Joe.'

'Maybe that's what you need,' Molly concedes before putting her arm around me. 'He seemed like a good lad while he was working for us, so I'm sure he will be a good husband to you. I wish you both well.'

'Thank you Molly. You're the first person to say that.'

'Being happy is the most important thing. But I agree with your parents, that boy had better look after you, and he's got some work to do to get everyone on side. Otherwise, your father is the least of his worries. He'll have me to answer to.'

I lean my head on Molly's shoulder. I know she means well but I also don't want to fall out with her about this. We sit together for a while, both lost in our own thoughts.

'Bread?' she says, breaking the silence.

'I thought you'd never ask,' I grin.

'Want some to take up for Owen?' Molly asks, as she hauls herself up and sets about slicing the freshly baked loaf.

'I'm sure he wouldn't say no,' I say, nabbing a piece for myself. 'I can't wait to introduce you to him properly.'

Molly seems pleased at this. 'You two come and have a cup of tea with me anytime.'

I taste a piece of the bread and it's every bit as delicious as I remember.

'Right, I better get on. I've got a cooked breakfast to make.'

'It's okay, I don't fancy a big breakfast today.'

'It's for our other guests.'

'Other guests?' I query. I assumed Owen and I would be the only ones staying here but, in the rush to put our travel plans together, it's not something I checked.

'There's an Italian couple staying. Very posh. Connections with royalty, I think.'

'I didn't realise there were bookings.'

'Well, you'd only just left. The management didn't think you'd be back again for a while.'

She's referring to my father's business directors, who are in charge of requests to stay on the island. Molly is very sceptical about Leo Harrison, my father's business protégé and the most recent addition to the management board. He seems to be pushing the island more as a way to gain favours for my father and also to generate even more revenue for the Barker-Jones empire, not that we really need it.

'They're leaving in a week, so they won't be here long,' Molly tells me.

'Okay, I'll let you get on then.' I plant a kiss on her powdery cheek and then retreat out of the kitchen. Looking over my shoulder as I'm leaving, I notice Molly is shaking her head. My heart sinks; I hope I haven't disappointed her or got her into too much trouble.

I'm sure she'll love Owen when she gets to know him. So I start thinking about how to introduce him in a way that will help to soften Molly's feelings towards him. Her approval means more to me than my father's.

Because I want my marriage to be perfect.

And I'm prepared to do whatever needs to be done to make that happen.

Chapter Five
Owen

'Now!' I shout and Sienna runs towards me, cutting through the water as quickly as she can. When she reaches me, I lift her up above my head and hold her there.

'We did it!' She giggles above me.

I let her down and we joke about how long it took us to achieve the iconic *Dirty Dancing* lift. It's been a good forty minutes or so and I feel a weird sense of accomplishment now we've got there. As we smooch in the sea, I wonder if this really is my life now. We've been here for almost a week and it's been absolute bliss. No more ten-hour working days, no more struggling to make ends meet. This is it. Just me and Sienna, here in the sunshine.

'Drink?' I ask her.

'Yes please, that was thirsty work.' Sienna lies down on a sunbed and picks up her paperback. I can tell she's about to settle into a leisurely reading session for the afternoon.

I saunter towards the little beach hut positioned part way along the bay. Jed is working there today. He's sitting on a bar stool, hunched over, tapping away on his mobile phone, and doesn't see me coming.

'Hey,' I say, not quite sure how to greet him. I haven't spoken to him properly since returning to Oyster Island and I'm keen to get the first awkward exchange done with.

'Oh, hi mate. How are you?' Jed stands up and shakes my hand.

'Not too bad,' I reply casually.

'Not too bad? Mate, you must be on top of the world right now!' He barks out a laugh. 'I mean...' He bobs his head in Sienna's direction. 'Well played, well played.' Jed shakes my hand again.

I shrug, not wanting to get too drawn into a conversation about Sienna.

'Drink?' Jed asks.

'Yeah, just two lemonades please.'

Jed pulls two glasses from the shelf and sets about filling them with ice and lemon. As he's preparing the drinks he says, 'I mean, you punched way above your weight. If I'd known Sienna was looking to hook up with one of the staff then...'

I clear my throat loudly and give him loaded look.

'Sorry, sorry,' Jed responds, not sounding sorry at all. 'Just impressed, you know. It's one thing having a summer fling with someone like that but getting married...' He puffs out his cheeks, then pours the ice-cold lemonade into the glasses. I'm keen to wrap up this conversation before it gets too personal.

'How did you do it?' Jed smirks but looks at me expectantly, as though I'm going to share tips with him.

'Jed, knock it off.' My voice is confident and firm. I'm Sienna's husband now, not the gardener. So I know I have to nip this kind of talk in the bud and make it clear that a line needs to be drawn.

Jed sneers and pushes the two glasses towards me. 'No worries, I know how it is. You're one of *the family* now.'

'Thanks,' I say as politely as I can manage. I take the glasses and make my way back towards my wife, annoyed that I didn't come up with a quick-witted comeback or a line to show Jed I'm not prepared to put up with his rudeness.

I'm keen to get the initial exchanges with staff out of the way. I want to try to strike a balance between still being friendly but making my position as Sienna's husband clear. Although I can see now that may be more difficult than I first thought. The way Jed said 'one of the family' made me feel uncomfortable. There was an undercurrent to his meaning I didn't like. I'm fully prepared to face a certain amount of dislike from those I worked shoulder to shoulder with. I was naive to think our marriage wouldn't change anything for me. There's going to be a certain amount of jealousy from people who see the wealth I've married into and are envious as a result.

'One lemonade.' I pass the drink over to Sienna and she gratefully takes a sip.

'Mmm, this tastes like Molly's homemade recipe.'

She sets her drink down on the low table next to her sunbed. 'I'm going to read a few more chapters,' she informs me before turning her attention back to the page in front of her.

I sit on the edge of my sunbed and stare out to sea. Being in the middle of the ocean, cut off from the rest of the world, isn't quite so appealing when coupled with the possibility that a number of people on the island may have ill feelings towards me. It can get pretty intense and claustrophobic being in the same place with the same people for a long stretch of time.

I may need to watch my back.

Because being associated with Sienna and her family could bring more risks than I'd realised.

Chapter Six
Sienna

'Who's that?' Owen asks.

Owen and I are once more swimming in the clear, aquamarine sea after a leisurely afternoon of sunbathing. I've stretched my body in the salty water and I'm starting to feel ready for a break from the sun. I shade my eyes and follow the direction his outstretched finger is pointing towards.

Two figures are standing on the sandy beach. I can just about make out that one is male and one female but we're too far out for me to distinguish any features. But it is clear they're not any of the staff, who all wear a uniform of a forest-green top and shorts. The pair on the beach are wearing swimwear.

'Um, not sure,' I say slowly. 'Maybe it's the Italian couple that Molly mentioned.'

'Could be,' Owen agrees. 'They seem to be waiting for us. Shall we swim back?'

I hesitate. I'm sure the people standing on the shore have a good reason to be there, and are completely harmless, but this island is meant to be my safe place. Two unknown figures are not part of my vacation plans. By now, I'm used to looking for danger wherever I go. I've had enough near misses to know that I have to be cautious where new people are concerned. Oyster Island is the one place where I don't have my security glued to my side. They're here on the island but not watching my every move as they do when I'm in England or America. I instinctively scan the bay, looking for Bruce and Kostas, the two stocky bodyguards who have been assigned to me for this trip. They've both been regular bodyguards of mine for many years. In fact, Bruce is one of our longest serving members of staff and he's been in my security team since I was a little girl. He's like an uncle to me. I catch sight of their bulky frames, clad in dark clothing, marching along the shoreline. Bruce is the older and taller of the two, he must be about six foot four, and he has long hair tied back into a ponytail. Kostas is shorter, just under the six foot mark, with close-cropped hair. I exhale; they've clocked the newcomers and are going to investigate themselves.

'Yes, let's see who they are.'

We take a gentle swim back towards the beach. I don't kick too hard as I want Bruce and Kostas to get to the unknown pair first. Sure enough, they reach them just as the two people are coming into focus. I don't recognise the woman. She looks about my age, with long, dyed silvery-coloured hair with a subtle purple balayage. She's wearing an all-in-one swimsuit that hugs her statuesque figure and a sarong is tied around her slim waist. I can see she's answering questions from my security duo without any hesitation. Next to her stands a person I recognise...

It's Leo Harrison. My father's business protégé and someone I know very well. He's an integral part of the majority of my father's business gatherings and has worked for the Barker-Jones empire for the last ten years. In the last eighteen months, he's been operating out of the Hong Kong office.

Bruce and Kostas back off. They know Leo and must be happy with his presence, so they retreat and sit on the low wall that separates the path from the beach.

'Sienna!' Leo raises a hand in greeting as I make my way across the beach. He picks up my beach towel from my sun lounger and tosses it towards me. I catch it, aware of Owen bristling behind me, and wrap the bright pink material around my body.

'Don't worry,' I say under my breath to Owen as he strides by my side. 'He works for my father.'

Owen's mouth is set in a straight line as he takes in this information and it's obvious my response isn't as reassuring as I'd intended it to be. At least he knows that Leo isn't some random intruder.

'Hey Leo,' I raise my voice and call over to him. He moves in our direction and the gap between us is quickly closed.

'What are you doing here?' I ask, wanting to find out exactly why Leo Harrison has come to Oyster Island. My mind is spinning and I wonder if my father has sent him out here to keep tabs on me and Owen. I can feel myself beginning to get mad at the idea but I want to give Leo the chance to tell me what's going on first.

'Just here for a break,' Leo remarks casually, running a hand through his light-brown hair.

'Nice to meet you.' He extends his other hand towards my husband. Owen grasps it in greeting and shakes it stiffly but doesn't say anything.

'Here for a break?' I question Leo. 'I don't think I've heard of you taking a vacation in all the time I've known you.'

'Exactly, it's about time I took a day off.' Leo smiles broadly. 'And while I'm here, I may put together some suggestions on how to make the most of this island.'

'Ah, thought so!' I exclaimed. 'Always working.' His reply has made me wonder if he's genuinely here to suss out the island but I'm still suspicious.

'What can I say, I can't help myself.' Leo flashes a grin at me. The conversation between us has been flying back and forth in that easy way that always happens whenever we're together.

'Anyway, what sort of changes are you talking about?' I press him, suddenly panicking he's about to turn this tranquil haven into some sort of tourist attraction.

'Nothing too major,' Leo says. 'It could just do with a few upgrades. Maybe a golf course and just a couple more villas.'

'Leo Harrison,' I say, poking him in the chest. 'Do not come here and start monetising my beautiful island—'

'I wouldn't dream of it,' Leo responds smoothly. 'It's just a few thoughts. I'll be running them past Derek of course.'

He sees the look on my face and then adds, 'And you too. If it's something you want to be involved in?'

Leo knows full well that I try to avoid any responsibilities connected to my father's business portfolios. But this is something I want a say in. The island means a lot to me.

'I think we're going to need to discuss this in more detail,' I say slowly, my brain already ticking over ideas on how I can show Leo that this island is perfect, just as it is. 'How long are you staying for?' I ask.

'A fortnight, maybe less. Depends how stir-crazy I go,' Leo jokes.

'And who's the lady with you?' Owen interrupts gruffly, tipping his head towards the woman still standing a few paces behind Leo.

'Oh sorry, my manners. This is Hazel Fanshawe.'

'Hi.' Hazel comes forward, flicking her styled hair over her shoulders. 'I'm Leo's girlfriend.'

'Welcome,' I say, although I'm almost speechless to discover that Leo, the eternal bachelor, now has a partner.

Hazel gives me a fake smile in response and I get the distinct vibe that she's completely uninterested in me. I take her in quickly, she's tall, elegant and clad head to toe in designer gear but even though she's ticking all the boxes for the type of person Leo might be attracted to for some reason I wouldn't have put the two of them together. Hazel is almost too glamorous, even for Leo.

Owen extends his hand, as though to shake Hazel's, but she blanks him and he awkwardly has to recover himself. I'm stunned by her rudeness. Then it occurs to me that I haven't actually introduced Owen.

'This is Owen Turner, my husband. We're on our honeymoon.'

'On honeymoon!' Leo seems taken aback. 'Are you serious?' He eyes up Owen. 'I thought he was one of your bodyguards.'

Owen half grunts beside me and I can tell he isn't happy Leo is here.

'Sorry,' Leo says, raising his hands to show he meant no offence. 'Congratulations to you both, that's wild news!'

'Did you really not know?' I ask, biting my lip.

'No, your father hadn't said anything.'

'Oh... so you're not here to spy on me then?'

'Spy on you? Leo snorts with laughter. 'Why would I spy on you?'

I rush to fill the gap, afraid of what Leo might say. Because he's known me for a long time and there's things I don't want him to mention in front of Owen.

'I thought Daddy might have sent you, to keep tabs on how things are going with my new husband.' I keep my eyes on Leo, watching to see if his reaction betrays any signs he's being untruthful.

'Nope, that's not the job Derek Barker-Jones employs me for.' Leo gives me a deadpan look.

'I'm sure you want to unpack,' I say pointedly, aiming to bring the conversation to a close. Having another couple on the island is the last thing I want on my honeymoon.

'Oh, we've already done that,' Leo says breezily. 'How about the four of us have drinks together later on? Maybe liven this place up a bit and raise a toast to your marriage?'

Hazel pouts, it seems this wasn't what she had in mind for her vacation either.

'I'm sure you'd rather settle into your accommodation.' I'm hoping Leo takes the hint that we'd rather not. After all, we've been on honeymoon for barely a week and I didn't intend to spend this time with anyone other than my husband.

'Nonsense. See you on the terrace at seven p.m.'

Leo is leaving before I can refuse. This is what he's like, full of arrogance, and he won't take no for an answer. His bullish attitude is exactly one of the reasons why my father rates him.

'Sorry,' I say to Owen, looping my arm into his. 'I can't believe Leo is here for a fortnight.'

Owen is still watching Leo as he disappears around the bend of the bay. I notice Leo and Hazel aren't holding hands or walking close to each other, there's quite a significant space between them. I wonder how long they've been together.

'Do you mind having a few drinks with them tonight?'

I can tell by the look on Owen's face that he does so I try to smooth the situation. 'We'll just spend this evening with them and then make it clear that we want some privacy.'

'I'm not sure you're going to get rid of that guy so easily,' Owen retorts.

I wish I could say he was wrong but Owen has quickly got the measure of Leo. And he's right, Leo isn't the sort of person you can shake off easily. I know, I've tried.

He's the last person I want to see on my honeymoon. Because Leo and I have more of a history than I'd like my husband to know about...

Chapter Seven
Owen

'To the married couple!'

I raise my drink towards the centre of the table and clink my glass with those of Sienna, Leo and Hazel. Tonight wasn't exactly what I had planned. We're on a private island and it didn't enter my head that we'd have any distractions on our honeymoon here. Earlier on I was annoyed that Sienna had agreed to socialising with the posh couple that turned up unexpectedly but, I have to admit that Leo has been a laugh so far. Plus, it's nice to be hanging out with people our age. I haven't had a proper night out since before I moved to Oyster Island for my gardening job and that was over six months ago now.

So much has changed since then. Including the freedom to go out for a spontaneous drink with friends. Maybe this is exactly what Sienna and I both needed. Some light-hearted socialising and to loosen up a little after the stress of being in her parents' London house. We've been completely wrapped up in each other since, but I know it's not healthy to spend all your time with just one person.

'Thanks,' I say, accepting another glass of wine. I've now warmed up a bit more to our surprise guests. Or maybe the alcohol I've been drinking has just relaxed me. I hadn't realised how tense I'd been feeling since staying with Sienna's parents. The whole experience was a bit of a disaster and I'm still trying to figure out how I can impress them enough to accept me as the person Sienna has chosen to spend the rest of her life with. In the next few months, Sienna and I will need to find ways to navigate our new life together and the pressure of that has been niggling away at me. It's time to let go of my worries and have some fun tonight.

We chat a bit more. Leo, with his upper-class accent, asks about my experience as a gardener and we exchange compliments about Oyster Island. He's not the sort of person I'd normally have a drink with but I'm going to be mixing with people in Sienna's circles more and more. I need to find some common ground with these filthy-rich, overconfident types. Behind her famous name and enormous privilege, Sienna is just another human being with her own vulnerabilities and hang-ups and I've more than connected with her. So I just need to remember this when I encounter the likes of Leo. He has a high-flying career, good looks and a fearless reputation, but he's still just another guy trying to make his mark on the world. Plus, I need to make an effort for Sienna's sake.

'How about some shots to really get things going?' Leo suggests.

'Count me in!' I reply, perhaps a little too eagerly.

'Shots! We're not in a club, Leo!' Sienna shrieks, giving away that she's already a little tipsy.

'Who cares!' Leo grins, and as he does so he casually places a hand on my wife's knee. It's only brief but I clock the action straight away. Instantly my guard is up again.

I hold my tongue and manage not to say anything. Perhaps Leo didn't mean to do it? Or maybe he's just smart and didn't leave his hand lingering for long enough to warrant me pulling him up on it.

Hazel is sitting next to me, opposite Leo. And from the pout of her mouth, she must have seen what just happened as well. She flounces off, in the direction of the bathroom, but Leo doesn't even look up. He just carries on chatting animatedly with my wife. They're now talking like there's no-one else in the room.

'Do you remember when—'

I tune out their exchange, they're reminiscing about mutual friends and I can't stand to keep listening in, all of a sudden feeling like a spare part to their cosy catch-up. I thought that Leo was an employee of Sienna's father's, not a good friend of hers. Or at least, that's how she made it sound when she introduced him earlier. Is that really true?

My memories drift to the last chat I had with my best mate, Darren. I video called him the day after Sienna and I got married, from a beach in Cuba. I remember switching the video in the direction of my new wife and Darren's response was something along the lines of: 'She's way out of your league!' He wasn't wrong and I'm well aware that Sienna is leagues above me in both looks and class. Darren continued to joke with me on the call, all in good humour, until later on in the conversation when I told him who Sienna was. I swore him to secrecy and he agreed. But I can't forget the troubled look on his face when he asked me, 'Are you sure you know what you're getting into?'

I brushed his concern off, my only thoughts of Sienna and the intense connection we'd formed. I'd not considered settling down before meeting her, always believing I was more of a free spirit. Meeting Sienna changed all that and I believed that our differences were a good thing. As the saying goes, opposites attract. Maybe I was being too naïve though. Her parents have already made their feelings clear and

I don't have any experience of interacting with people like Leo and Hazel. Well, except from being paid to do their dirty work for them.

Sienna calls my name and I jerk back into the present moment. 'Leo has twisted my arm; do you want a shot as well?' She flutters her eyelids prettily at me.

'Go on then,' I say, making an effort to join in once more and trying to push aside my worries. I'm on edge and way out of my comfort zone. I just need to chill out a bit.

Jed arrives with a tray full of little glasses. I inwardly curse that it's him again. But, on such a small island, I know I'm going to be seeing a lot of the same faces.

'Here we go,' he says, setting the tray down on the table between us. 'Can I get you anything else?'

'I think these will be more than enough,' Sienna says, not even giving Jed a passing glance.

There's something in her tone that's quite dismissive and I notice she doesn't even say thank you. I've not really witnessed how she behaves around the staff. When we met, we were outside in the early morning and she was obviously attracted to me from the start. After that, we met in secret, sneaking around at night-time or meeting in quiet places where we knew we'd be unlikely to be seen. It's understandable that her behaviour towards me was different, we were falling for each other and I guess I wasn't just another person at her beck and call. Right now, I feel embarrassed about the way she's interacted with Jed, so I step in and do the honours instead.

'Thanks mate,' I say to Jed.

I'm expecting him to react positively to my acknowledgement of his work but, instead, he looks between me and Sienna and gives me a little smirk. He turns and leaves us to it. I have a sinking feeling that I've done something wrong. And I make a mental note to work out how to strike the right balance between being polite to the staff but also not too friendly.

Leo hands me a shot and I down it immediately.

'Woah, steady on old man,' Leo winks at me. There's something about his polished accent that gets under my skin. I ignore him and swipe another shot. After all, it would be a pity to see them go to waste.

Sienna and Leo clink their little glasses. Leo cries, 'To vacations!' and Sienna echoes his sentiments. She pulls a face as the bitter taste hits her tongue.

'Urgh, that's strong!'

And she's right, whatever the liquor in the shot glasses is, it's pretty potent. I can't quite place my finger on what exactly it is, but I'm sure it's something expensive and therefore I'm not going to put my foot in it and show my ignorance. It all does the same job, no matter how much money it costs.

'So where did you two get married then?' Leo enquires. 'You certainly struck while the iron was hot,' he leans towards me conspiratorially. 'Fair play.'

I don't know why I'm taking everything the wrong way tonight. I guess this kind of scenario is all new to me and I'm wary about how to present myself in this unfamiliar landscape. The truth is, I feel worried about putting a foot wrong. I want Sienna to be proud of me and to see me as her equal. So, with that thought in mind, I try to shed my grizzly bear attitude and go for a comeback that will appease Sienna but show Leo I'm onto him.

'Well, you wouldn't want to let someone as special as Sienna slip through your fingers...'

His reaction is as predicted. Leo sits back, no doubt analysing me and wondering how on earth a guy like me ended up marrying a woman like her. He pushes another shot glass towards me and flashes his perfect white smile.

'That's so cute,' Sienna says. And then she launches into a detailed run-down of our wedding day. She gushes about our vows and how unique our intimate ceremony was. Listening to her speaking helps to smooth some of my doubts.

'It was just magical. More perfect than I could ever have imagined.' Sienna leans across the table and entwines my hand with hers, her engagement ring shimmering under the outdoor lighting.

I kiss her hand and wish that we could go back to being just the two of us. Things are far less complicated when it's just me and her. But I know that's not real life.

Hazel eventually rejoins our group and sits on the edge of the conversation, obviously still moody with Leo. Although, I don't blame her because her boyfriend continues to be very familiar with Sienna, draping his arm over the back of her chair and turning towards her to whisper things that only she can hear. I don't want to appear jealous in the way Hazel does. I try to tell myself that I'm probably being paranoid and oversensitive.

'So how did you and Leo meet?' I ask Hazel, in an attempt to get to know her.

She narrows her green cat's eyes at me. 'We met through mutual friends.' She pauses and then smiles sweetly at me. 'And how did you meet Sienna?'

It's clear she knows and I think she's trying to trip me up. Why is tonight turning out to be so much of a disaster? Am I so obviously a working-class guy who doesn't belong here? I feel like a complete fish out of water.

'We met here, on the island,' I gesture to the setting around me. 'I can't think of a more romantic place to fall in love, can you?'

I know it's mushy, but I mean it sincerely. And I want everyone to realise that I do really care for Sienna.

'It's certainly very impressive,' Hazel replies.

Sienna laughs loudly at another one of Leo's jokes and I feel myself tensing up even more, trying not to stare in a hostile way across the table at the man I'm fast coming to think of as my rival. The way Sienna's tilting her head towards him as he speaks and playing with her long, golden hair isn't something that I feel comfortable with either. From where I'm sitting, it looks as though they're both flirting with each other. Perhaps this is how Sienna behaves when she's with other men... I wouldn't know as I haven't experienced this kind of situation with her before. Perhaps I'm overthinking things and I just need to relax.

I keep drinking, hoping it will blot out my fears.

It doesn't help though. If anything, the alcohol makes my head ache ever more. All I can think of, as the night wears on, is whether Darren was right. Can I really fit into Sienna's high-class world? Can I live up to her family's expectations? Am I enough?

Or have I made the biggest mistake of my life?

Chapter Eight
Sienna

'So, tell me, what are you really planning?' I smile encouragingly at Leo, hoping my direct approach combined with my mischievous expression will get him to open up about what he's really doing on the island.

Leo runs a hand through his short brown hair, a familiar action I've seen a thousand times before. I can tell he's weighing up how to answer me.

He's mostly probed me for information this evening, asking about how Owen and I met, what our wedding day was like and if we have any plans for the future. I've answered all these questions with the expectation that Leo is going to divulge some, if not all, of what he learns to my father.

This is because Leo has always been a 'yes man', dancing to my father's tune. That's why he's got as far as he has in his career at such a young age. He's prepared to do what needs to be done to get ahead. It's something I learned the hard way about him.

I brush thoughts of our past interactions aside and clasp my hands together, waiting to hear what he has to say.

'This island, it costs a lot of money to run.'

I'm well aware of this already, although I've never really been interested in the financial running of my father's businesses. It's something I've had an active disinterest in, much to the annoyance of both of my parents. It seems as though now might be the time to get clued up; if my unspoilt island is at risk then I need knowledge on my side to try to figure out how to save it.

'Derek is starting to look ahead to his retirement—'

'His retirement?' I choke in disbelief. The idea of my father ever retiring from the hustle and bustle of running his various media empires seems absurd to me.

'I'm serious,' Leo insists. 'He wants to wind down, enjoy his silver years.'

'My father wants to wind down?' I repeat. 'Has he actually said that to you?'

'Not in so many words, but his actions speak for him.'

'And where does the island come in?'

'Well it takes a number of staff to run, which is an expense in itself, not to mention the upkeep.' Leo sweeps one arm out wide as if to demonstrate the magnitude of what's involved and then leans back, allowing his other arm to drape along the back of my chair.

Leo's getting a little close for comfort, but it feels like he's about to reveal some useful facts to me, so I stay where I am, not wanting to break the flow of his words.

'So Derek is considering whether to scale back in terms of the team that's here or to go in the other direction.'

'Elaborate,' I say firmly, starting to get impatient at the way Leo is spinning this out.

Leo sits up straight now. 'He's looking at whether to turn the place into a more exclusive resort. Interest in staying here is increasing, as word gets around and the right people start to notice what an incredible location this is. In the last year, more and more of your father's contacts have been asking to vacation here. Currently, he can only approve so many of those who are keen to visit because of the limited accommodation. Plus, he wants to improve the facilities for those who do spend time here.'

'I see. So it's about using the island to gain more favour with his contacts... and those he wants to be more connected with?'

'Something like that,' Leo concedes.

'And I'm guessing the golf course is for my father's retirement?'

'Knowing your father, I'd say so.'

I sigh. My father never spent any of the long school summer breaks out here with me and my mother when I was growing up. He was always too busy working on projects that were far too important for him to step away from to spend some time with us. Yet, he's quite happy to ensure his business contacts have updated facilities put in place. And, if there's a golf course out here, even if we did end up having a vacation as a family, I'm sure my father would spend more time hitting a ball than he would with me.

'What's bothering you so much? Isn't it about time the island had an upgrade?'

'I like it as it is,' I huff. For me, this island is the one place that never seems to change. It holds precious memories of me and my mother actually spending time together. As well as countless time spent here with Molly and Joseph in more recent years and the destination where I met the love of my life.

It's more than that though, it's the one place where I get to be myself. I'm not crowded by security and I can run free, on this unspoilt island. Yes, the villa and the other buildings are starting to get a bit dated now but I hate the thought of it all changing. This place is the connection between my past and present, the place I associate with my childhood and a raft of happy memories.

'It's going to happen, Sienna,' Leo says, his voice softer and more gentle than usual. 'You know what Derek is like, so it's best to get used to the idea.'

He's right, but I don't want to accept it just yet. I turn my attention to Owen but he's chatting away to Hazel and I decide not to interrupt. I don't know Hazel at all, although the Fanshawe surname rings a bell for some reason. I can't think why...

Hazel is constantly flicking her hair, it seems to be her thing. Or perhaps she just likes to draw attention to the expensive cut. She's wearing a tight, pale pink body-con dress that doesn't leave much to the imagination. I'm intrigued that Leo has a girlfriend. He's not usually the commitment type, so I'm curious to find out all about the person who has finally pinned him down and put a label on him. However, the night is still young and I'm keen for Owen to make friends, so I leave him to it. I'm sure there will be plenty of time to talk with Hazel later.

I pick up my glass of gin and tonic and move to the terrace railings, leaning on them and drinking in the gorgeous scenery. This sea view is one of the best on the island, which is no doubt why my mother instructed for this villa to be built here over thirty years ago. This vacation home was a wedding present from my father to my mother.

She loves this space as dearly as I do. Although, I suspect it's because it's her avenue of escape from her marriage.

It's not that my parents don't get on, they do. Sometimes I think they're too similar. Except, my father is really full on. He never stops, jumping from one project to another, spearheading new ways of doing things and driving more and more revenue for his multitude of businesses. They talk business a lot, which is understandable given how integral my father's success is to our family life. But they're not romantic with each other. They're friends, allies, team players, but they don't have that spark between them.

Leo comes and stands next to me. 'It's a beautiful evening.'

'It sure is. Don't you think the island looks stunning, just the way it is?'

'Hey,' Leo puts his hands up in defence. 'It's not me that you have to convince.'

'No, but I'm guessing you might be project managing the whole thing so you'll have some influence.'

'Possibly, it hasn't been confirmed yet.'

'But it's likely,' I press.

'Depending on a few things.'

'What things?' My interest is piqued. Even though Leo protested earlier that he wasn't here to spy on me, I'm still not convinced that's true.

'Boring business things,' Leo jokes. He falls quiet, staring out to sea.

I'm now bristling with annoyance at the possibility my father has sent Leo here on purpose to keep tabs on me. Even if Leo doesn't think that's why my father has dispatched him here on a new project to renovate the island, the fact Leo's visit just happens to coincide with my honeymoon is too much of a coincidence. Because if there's one thing I know about my parents, it's that they like to have control of what's going on in my life. And that's why this whole situation with Owen has angered them so much.

If I'm being honest, deep down, my rush to marry Owen may also have been a lot to do with gaining some actual control over my own life and wanting to make my own choices. Of course I've fallen for him, there's no doubt about that, but the hasty marriage was also a victory for me. I still can't quite believe that my parents didn't get wind of what was going on and that we managed to tie the knot without them interfering in our plans. I can't help but smile at knowing I've won this battle... for now.

Owen is drinking his wine and, as I look at him dressed in his Ralph Lauren t-shirt and the denim shorts he bought in Cuba, my heart beats a little faster. He's classically tall, dark and handsome. He ticks all the boxes for me, but whereas before I'd always gone for tall and skinny types, Owen is broad-shouldered. He is muscular from all the outdoor work he used to do and he likes to keep up his weight training as well.

An idea enters my head, I turn it over and over. Perhaps it's the alcohol but I wonder if there's a seed of something in it. Owen knows this island. As a gardener he got to grips with it pretty quickly. If my father is set on changing this place, then maybe, just maybe, I could suggest that Owen and I are part of the updates. That way, Owen can get involved in something that's more in his comfort zone and I can try to steer the project in a direction that doesn't change things too drastically.

I sip my drink and congratulate myself on the thought. It would solve so many problems. My father will be pleased that I'm taking an interest in one of his business ventures and it might enable Owen to form a positive bond with my parents. I feel a bubble of excitement rise inside me and I can't wait to share the suggestion with Owen.

My husband is still talking with Hazel. She seems to be chilling out more now and her stiff demeanour has fallen away. Leo is still standing at my side, and there's no denying he's attractive. He has the beginnings of a tan, he's lean and athletic, and he has cute dimples in his cheeks. Flashbacks of the past overwhelm me. Images of me and Leo, a few years ago when things were very different. But anything that was between us is in the past now. I'm happily married and Leo has moved on as well.

All my life, I've wished for a marriage based on love, rather than a marriage of convenience and social standing, which is the arrangement my parents have. Leo Harrison would have been the perfect son-in-law for Derek Barker-Jones. In many ways, committing to Owen, who's the polar opposite to Leo in every respect, is perhaps my means of rebelling against the path my parents had set out for me.

Although, it's hard to rebel against an upbringing like mine. I have nothing to be ungrateful for. Yet, everything has been so controlled, so ordered, that I longed to be free, to be someone other than me for a day. I wanted to meet someone who doesn't look past me and see my father's power or money, to run wild without two burly middle-aged men protecting my every move. And I dreamt of falling in love with someone who has no knowledge of my family, someone who just wanted to be with me for me.

'You know, I was surprised to hear of your nuptials like that.' Leo leans towards me once more, talking in a low voice and interrupting my thoughts.

'You really hadn't been told by my parents?' Heat rises in my cheeks. I wasn't expecting to encounter Leo again before the news of my wedding had circulated more widely.

'It took me by surprise. The last time we saw each other, I—'

'Leo,' I say sharply. My voice carries further than I meant it to.

'Oh my God!' Hazel leaps to her feet and a dark red stain is spreading across her blush-coloured dress. 'What the hell are you doing?' she rages, her question directed at Owen.

Owen looks bleary-eyed and tries to stutter a reply, but his words come out all jumbled at first. 'I'm sorry,' he slurs. 'I knocked over my wine.'

The red liquid has run across the table and gone all over Hazel.

'Do you know how much this dress cost?' Hazel cries, 'It's one of a kind!'

Owen grabs a napkin from in front of him and stands up, moving towards Hazel, but as he does so he staggers and trips over his own feet. One minute he is upright, and the next he is crashing to the ground.

'Owen! Owen, are you okay?' I rush over to him, at first worried that he's smacked his head on the cold, unforgiving tiles on the terrace.

I kneel down beside him and begin to check him over.

I'm mortified when he starts laughing. Not quietly, but loud blasts of laughter, interspersed with hiccups.

'Owen...' I'm lost for words. I don't want to look up and see Leo and Hazel's pitying expressions so I stay where I am, wanting the floor to swallow me up.

How did he get so drunk? I know we're all a bit tipsy, but surely he knows his own limits?

He slurs my name and attempts to move, only to fall back down again.

I'm really worried about him but, at the same time, I can't help also feeling embarrassed.

'Come on, let's get you up,' Leo says authoritatively, stepping in to help. He calls over the waiter who's been serving us this evening and they both manage to set Owen back on his chair. My husband continues to laugh.

A creeping sense of doubt begins to wash over me. My parents' misgivings ringing in my ears.

Do I really know Owen well enough?

And is this just a one-off? Or a taste of what's to come?

Chapter Nine
Owen

I don't like the way my wife is looking at me.

This is my first thought as I wake up this morning. My eyes feel gritty and heavy and it's a huge effort just to peel them open. My throat is raw, as though I've been shouting. And my emotions are all over the place after a night of fitful dreams.

Why is Sienna staring at me with such a disdainful look on her face?

'Owen, are you okay?' she asks tentatively, handing me a mug of steaming, freshly brewed coffee.

'Water, I need water,' I croak, passing the hot mug back to her.

She pours me a glass and hands it to me. I gratefully swig the ice-cold liquid. And then I remember. The events of last night all come flooding back to me.

'Oh... Sienna, I don't know what came over me.' I reach for her hand and pull her closer to me. 'I'm sorry. Did I make a complete fool of myself?'

She remains silent, and the absence of comforting words speaks volumes to me. After a few beats, she says, 'How did you get so drunk?'

'Sienna, the shots. Leo kept passing them over to me and they were pretty strong. I don't think I've tasted anything like it before!'

Her serious expression melts away. 'So you didn't get drunk on purpose then?'

'No! Why would I do that? I just hadn't eaten much and it's been a while since I've consumed that amount of alcohol.'

Sienna sighs and comes to lie next to me on the bed. The sunlight falls through the curtains and onto the section of the bed where Sienna is stretched out, she looks truly beautiful. The morning light falling on her in this way reminds me of the days when we woke up to see the sun rise together on her boat as we made our way towards Cuba, and to married life. I prop myself up on an elbow and my brain gradually begins to kick into gear.

'Wait, you mean you were worried that you'd married a secret alcoholic?'

Sienna blushes.

I groan loudly. 'Damn, I really did make a fool of myself, didn't I?'

'Just a bit.'

'I promise you now, my only issue with drink is my low tolerance. I'm not a regular drinker, so last night was a lot for me... What was that stuff, anyway?'

'Curaçao liqueur. It's a Caribbean drink.'

I trace my finger along Sienna's jawline and feel her visibly relax.

'I'm sorry, I'll try not to let it happen again.' I lean over to kiss her.

She pulls back from me though, her blue eyes flashing at me.

'What's the matter?'

'Try? I'd rather it didn't happen again.' Her voice is hard and cool. 'And I suggest you brush your teeth.'

Wow, I can't believe how she shot me down so quickly.

'Sienna—' I attempt to reassure her but she stands up and makes for the bedroom door.

'I'm going for breakfast,' she says, her tone still steely.

'Well, I need to sleep this off,' I reply slowly. My instincts are screaming at me to accompany her to breakfast and to nip this misunderstanding in the bud. But I don't feel well at all and it would be better if I tackled this situation with a clear head. Otherwise, I'm just going to keep making things worse.

Sienna stalks out of the room and shuts the door firmly.

I fall back onto the soft pillow, annoyed at myself for creating this situation. I stare up at the ceiling, the room around me feeling like it's spinning. Reaching over to the bedside table, I stretch towards the glass of water. But I misjudge it and the glass topples. I watch in slow motion as it wobbles for a split second and then tumbles to the floor. That's the second time in twenty-four hours that I've knocked something over.

I groan out loud before peering over the edge of the bed to assess the damage. The glass has shattered and the water is pooling across the tiled floor. Slumping back into the sumptuous four-poster bed, I don't have the energy to start sweeping up pieces of broken glass. So I leave the wreckage where it is, planning to tidy up later. At least the water will soon dry up, as the temperature is likely to be high again today.

Still feeling thirsty, I lie in a daze. Not quite awake but not quite asleep either. In one of those horrible limbo states where you should be resting but your body is on high alert.

I begin to spiral into a panicked state. Coming back to Oyster Island was meant to be a chance for Sienna and me to get to know each other even better and to create memories to last a lifetime. I was also grateful to get a reprieve after the disastrous introduction to her parents. I'm starting to worry that I'm just not cut out for this kind of life. But then I think of Sienna and all the time we've spent, content in each other's company. That's something worth fighting for. I resolve to be honest and to share my anxieties with Sienna. Maybe that way she'll see the circumstances from my point of view and understand I'm nervous about meeting the people in her life who are important to her. It means everything to me that I make a go of this. I just hope that Sienna can see that, even if I'm making mistakes, I'm trying my best.

***

The sheets are tangled round my legs and my torso is hot and sweaty. I sit bolt upright. I must've fallen back to sleep and I don't know how long I've been in bed for. Scrambling around, I find my smartwatch under one of the pillows.

'Aarrg!' The watch is showing after midday. I can't believe I've slept for so many hours.

I swing up and out of bed.

Crunch. My right foot goes straight in the broken glass that I left scattered over the floor earlier.

I curse, multiple times. And then, wincing, I bring my right foot up to rest on my knee and assess the damage.

It could be a lot, lot worse. But it's still not ideal.

I brush a few bigger shards from the sole of my foot and they come off easily. Looking closer, I can now see several smaller pieces of glass that are wedged further into my skin and my little toe is bleeding a fair amount.

I'm not quite sure how I'm going to explain this to Sienna. Things really aren't going my way. I gingerly inch off the bed and then hop on my left foot towards the balcony doors. I scan outside but I can't see anyone nearby. I don't want to call Sienna and bother her with this. I was hoping a member of staff might be around to help me, but I don't seem to be in luck.

I hop back inside and sit down in a fawn-coloured armchair positioned by one of the floor-length windows. I get to work on picking out the tiny pieces of glass, gently easing them one by one from the bottom of my foot.

Part way through my task, there's a knock at the door.

'Room service!' a male voice calls.

'Come in,' I say gruffly.

The door opens and it's none other than Jed.

'Hi, Sienna said to bring in something to eat if you hadn't appeared by midday.' He indicates to the tray laden with croissants.

Jed's eyebrows are slightly raised and I feel like I'm being gently told off for sleeping in. He starts to walk towards the bedside table.

'Stop!' I warn him. 'There's broken glass on the floor there. I knocked a drink over.'

'Good job I got you another one then.'

'Yes, appreciated,' I reply in a level voice. And then decided to change tack, because I don't want to pretend to be someone I'm not.

'Look, let's cut the crap Jed.' I pause. 'Can you clean up the mess on the floor please and try not to mention it again.'

'Certainly, *sir*.' He sets the tray down.

'Jed, look I don't know why you're acting like this. Surely it's worth your while to at least try to be civil to me?'

'Now you're the big shot, you mean?' His mouth is set in a grimace as he says this.

'No! That's not what I mean at all.'

Jed gives me another one of his smirks. 'My employer is Derek Barker-Jones, he's still the man who pulls all the strings.'

I understand where Jed is coming from. He can't see me being a favourite of Derek's, so therefore he doesn't care about being antagonistic towards me. However, he does get a dustpan and brush and begins to sweep away the mess I've created.

Inspecting my foot more closely, I can see there's still two or three tiny shards of glass that I haven't been able to pull out.

Reluctantly, I gesture to my foot and ask Jed, 'Is there anyone who can come and take a look at this?'

He straightens up, 'Of course. I'll be back with someone shortly.'

I exhale with relief that he hasn't made another sarcastic comment. My head is pounding and I can't take trying to work out mind games today.

'Hello, what's the matter then?' Molly bustles into the room. It's the first time I've seen her since I've returned to the island not as an employee. Molly and Joseph are the most senior staff on the island and they run a tight ship.

'Hi Molly,' I say pleasantly, glad to see her. She's a kind woman and we've previously got on well. 'Glass in my foot,' I tell her.

Molly bends down and quickly assesses the damage. 'We'll need some tweezers to pull that one out.' As she says this, she manages to dislodge a further piece of glass from my skin. 'And a plaster for that toe. Do you think you can make your way downstairs for me?'

'Yes,' I say, standing up awkwardly. We make our way to the lift and down to the ground floor. There, Molly shows me into a small, light-filled room off the hallway that I didn't know existed. There's a single bed in here, with pristine white sheets, and a number of cupboards. Molly pulls out a first aid kit and sets to work.

'There you go,' she says with a satisfied smile on her face. 'All patched up in no time.'

'Thank you.'

'Now, let me make you a coffee.'

'You don't have to do that,' I insist. It feels strange to have my former boss offering to make me a drink.

Molly eyes me up. 'You'll have to get used to the change in dynamics soon enough,' she remarks. 'And I want to have a word with you as well...'

Her sentence hangs in the air between us as Molly leads me out of the small room and towards the expansive kitchen.

I brace myself for the conversation to come. I'm sure Molly wants to have her say about me abandoning my job to run off and get married to the heiress.

Molly fires up a coffee machine. I notice there's a strawberry cheese-cake sitting on the worktop beside it. It looks as though she was half way through decorating the top. Judging by Molly's cooking so far, I'm sure it's going to be every bit as delicious as it looks.

'Sugar?' she asks.

'Just one.'

'Sit.' Molly points to the farmhouse-style table in the middle of the room.

I gingerly sit down on the chair, my foot still stinging slightly.

'Now,' the older woman says, setting my coffee in front of me. 'Let's have a little chat.'

I hold my breath.

'First of all, congratulations.'

'Thanks,' I stutter, not sure what to expect from this exchange.

'Second of all, and most important, make sure you look after Sienna.' There's a tone to her voice that tells me she means business.

'I promise I will.'

'That girl means the world to me.' There's a sincere look on her lined face.

'And to me,' I say, with as much feeling as I can muster. I want to convince Molly that my intentions towards Sienna are pure.

'Well, as long as you stick to that promise, we'll get along just fine.' Molly gives me a small smile.

'I understand,' my words come out in a rush. 'I know what some people must be thinking of me. But I didn't realise who she was at first. We just clicked and everything that happened afterwards felt right.'

'You don't have to explain yourself.' Molly blows on her hot coffee.

'But I want to.'

Molly laughs. 'I've known Sienna since she was a tiny tot. If she'd set her sights on you then nothing was going to get in her way. I'm pleased she's looking happy. But you've got some hard work ahead of you with her parents, you know that?'

I nod, fully aware of the monumental challenge in front of me.

'I better get on.' Molly stands up, making it clear our little chat has come to an end. She returns to decorating her cheesecake.

'Thanks for the coffee and for sorting my foot,' I say as I leave.

My head feels slightly clearer now. I plan to go and take a shower and then find my wife.

As I climb up the twisting staircase, Jed is making his way down it.

'Glass all sorted,' he says.

'Cheers.' I keep walking past him.

'By the way, if you're looking for Sienna...' Jed leaves the sentence hanging and I'm forced to turn back to show him I want to know more. 'She's out on a speedboat with Leo Harrison.'

I would love to wipe the smug expression off Jed's face right now. It's obvious he's trying to wind me up, so I make sure to keep my cool and thank him.

But I'm anything but cool and collected. The thought of Leo getting close to Sienna on a boat out in the ocean makes me want to throw up. I march back to our room, where I dress and shower hurriedly.

I'm going to find Sienna.

And when I see Leo, I'm going to make it clear I'm not the sort of guy he can cross.

Chapter Ten
Sienna

I stomp down the stairs, away from Owen in his hungover state. When I get to the bottom step, I hesitate. I want to go back up to him. I hate that we've just been prickly with each other and I don't like walking away from him while I'm feeling like this. I should go back to the bedroom, so we can kiss and make up and spend the rest of the morning in bed together.

Through the window, I can see the sky is bright and inviting. So I settle on going for a quick stroll first, to blow the cobwebs away and to put myself into a better mood. I always feel more positive after stretching my legs and clearing my mind. It's probably best to let Owen have a bit more of a sleep as well. He looked pretty ashen-faced and I'm sure the alcohol was still pumping through his system.

I cast my thoughts back to last night. Owen did have a few shots in quick succession but I didn't think he was drinking huge amounts more than the rest of us. That's why I was so confused when he fell over. I didn't see his accident coming. Conjuring up his face and his words from this morning, I feel more reassured that it was simply a case of him not being used to the strong measures. I'll have to try to remember that for the future. Although I don't think we will be drinking like that again anytime soon.

I make my way out of the perimeter of the villa and down the hill, breathing in the fresh lemon-scented air.

'Hey Sienna!'

I spin on my heels, hoping Owen has followed me. But it's not Owen. It's Leo.

'How are you this morning?'

'Fine, thanks.'

'And Owen?' There's mischief in Leo's expression.

'As you'd expect, he's not in the best state,' I cut him off and carry on walking, because I'm not really in the mood to stand around chatting.

'Sienna, do you fancy coming out in the speedboat with us?' Leo asks.

I stop. Leo draws level with me and, out of the corner of my eye, I can see Hazel trailing behind us. She's wearing high wedge sandals, which aren't very practical on the uneven ground here.

'I thought it might be fun to have a zoom around the island.'

I have to admit, it's tempting. It's been a while since I've been on a speedboat around Oyster Island. I bite my lip, considering the offer.

'Go on, you know you want to,' Leo encourages me.

I fiddle with my charm bracelet. All I really want to do is go back to my room and dive under the duvet with Owen. However, it would be another opportunity to find out more details from Leo about how far along the plans for the island are. Now that I've come to terms with the idea that the development is very likely to go ahead, I want to ensure the updates aren't too extensive and don't make Oyster Island completely unrecognisable. I'm keen to work out ways in which Owen and I could be involved in the project and this would mean I could gather more information before I surprise him with the idea. I really hope he is on board with the suggestion.

'Okay. When are you setting off?'

'Now,' Leo responds. 'No time like the present.'

He offers me an arm, but I decline. Hazel is still a few paces behind us and I'd feel odd hanging off Leo's arm when Hazel is clearly more in need of the support.

'Your girlfriend could do with someone to lean on,' I whisper under my breath.

We both stop and allow Hazel to catch us up.

'Are you all right in those shoes?' I enquire. 'The ground gets even more bumpy further down the slope.'

Hazel pouts, unimpressed.

'Come here,' Leo says.

Hazel leans heavily on Leo. 'Shall I get someone to run back for your flats?' he asks.

'That might be a good idea, given how bad the paths are here.' she remarks loudly.

'You see, this is the sort of thing that could do with improving.' Leo says pointedly.

'The cobbles and the dirt tracks add to the charm of the island.' I insist.

'They could also become a headache if someone falls and files a lawsuit for tripping and breaking a leg,' Leo shoots back.

'Always so practical,' I remark.

'That's me,' Leo says, choosing to take this as a compliment.

'Well, the current pathways could be improved,' I concede, taking a hairband from my wrist and tying up my long locks. 'But no new ones.'

Leo doesn't answer, which makes me think that plans are probably further along than he's letting on. And that I definitely need to see what he and my father have been plotting.

'Who's coming out on the boat with us?' I ask.

'Just me and Hazel.'

'Are you driving?'

'Yeah, it's my speedboat.' There's a natural charm that borders on arrogance in everything Leo says, but for the most part he manages to pull it off.

'I'm going to need security with me. And I'd rather Joseph was in charge of the vessel.' I'm surprised Leo hasn't thought about this, he knows how strict my parents' rules are around my safety.

'Of course,' Leo is gracious in defeat. 'I'll go and find them.'

'Don't forget to bring my sandals as well,' Hazel reminds him.

'Wouldn't dream of it,' Leo winks at her but she doesn't respond, so he turns to walk back up the hill.

That leaves me and Hazel standing together, in the shade of a palm tree. She looks bored, her mouth downturned, not like someone who's enjoying a vacation with her partner.

'How are you finding Oyster Island?'

'I can see why Leo has plans to improve it,' Hazel replies instantly. She's picking at her manicured nails and unaware of how her words land with me. 'The views are pretty though and the food has been amazing.'

'I'm impressed that you've managed to get Leo to go on a holiday.' I choose my words carefully and I'm intrigued to see how she responds.

Hazel looks at me, her green eyes hard. 'I don't think Leo sees it as a holiday, it's a work trip really.'

'I thought as much,' I mumble under my breath.

A silence hangs between us. Hazel makes no attempt to further the conversation and so I turn my attention to the sea. It shimmers in the sunshine and looks so inviting. I can't wait to get out on the water.

Leo comes back down the hill, accompanied by a willowy blonde dressed in the forest-green uniform of the staff. She's clutching a pair of flat sandals. The woman is our newest member of staff but I've never met her before. As the woman hands over the sandals to Hazel, I observe her. She's the same height as me and our hair colour is almost a perfect match. I make a mental note of the name on her badge – Astrid – before she moves off discreetly. I like to know the names of everyone working on Oyster Island, from the women in the laundry to the fishermen. It's just one of the ways I feel connected to this place.

'Joseph and Bruce are both coming,' Leo confirms. 'They'll be with us soon.'

We continue along to the jetty area, where Leo's very large speed-boat is moored. It's a pricey model and it makes the basic fishermen's boats along the harbour look even more rustic. It also has me wondering what kind of salary my father is paying Leo now. I'm sure his numbers have been on the rise, along with his importance, since the work he completed in Hong Kong. By all accounts, Leo made some lucrative deals and set up some important opportunities, just as my father had wanted. The Barker-Jones name is prominent in the media industry in the Western world but my father has been trying to make a name for himself in East Asia for a long time.

'Hong Kong was a success then?' I probe. We leave Hazel changing into her flat sandals and walk together until we reach the end of the jetty.

Leo has a sad expression on his face. 'It was a success in business terms, yes. Your father was very pleased but... I would never have gone if I'd known...'

Inhaling sharply, I grab Leo's hand and pull him onto the deck of the boat. 'Leo, let's not mention...'

'Sienna, how can you expect me not to ask you what happened?'

The elephant has finally come crashing into the room.

'You chose to go to Hong Kong.'

'I thought we had an understanding. I thought you'd wait for me.'

Leo's hand is still in mine. I drop the connection and create some physical space between us.

'Leo, you said you were going for six months. You were there for over eighteen... did you think I wouldn't move on?'

'What we had – what we have – is unique. So, yes, I thought we had a future.'

'I barely heard from you while you were over there.'

'You stopped receiving my calls!' Leo's voice is rising now.

'We hadn't seen each other in almost a year!' I match him in volume, angry at all he put me through. All the lonely nights when I wondered if he ever really cared for me at all.

Leo shakes his head. 'I knew I should've come back.'

I can't believe he is saying all of this. If I'd heard these words from Leo Harrison over a year ago then things might have turned out differently. But he put work before me, just like my father has always done. He decided his path when he extended his stay in Hong Kong and he made it clear I wasn't his first priority at the time. In the last few years, I've come to understand myself better and I'm not prepared to be anyone's second priority.

Ducking into the cabin, I try to hide my tears. A storm of emotions has kicked up inside me. Leo's saying all of the right things, but it's too little and it's far too late. Part of me feels sorry for what might've been but I know I've given my heart to someone who adores me.

'Sienna, listen.' Leo has followed me and it's clear he doesn't want to drop this.

'Stop Leo. Your girlfriend is just out there and I'm a married woman. It's not appropriate to be talking like this now. It's in the past.'

'Hazel may be my girlfriend,' Leo spits, 'But she's nothing compared to you.'

I roll my eyes.

'I mean it, Hazel did all the chasing. We haven't been together that long and I'm not serious about her.'

'Don't lead her on then! Whatever Hazel is to you is not my concern.' I break eye contact with him.

'When you stopped returning my calls... I was at a low point. That's the only reason...'

'Don't!' I can't listen to what Leo has to say. He's the only man I've loved apart from Owen and this conversation is stirring up too many old feelings.

'I still love you.'

My heart skips a beat. Why is he doing this now?

Before I can answer, Joseph appears on board the boat with Hazel and Bruce in tow. I pray that she hasn't overheard our exchange. I rush down the small set of steps to the tiny bathroom to compose myself. It takes a few minutes to regain control of my emotions. Dabbing my eyes and straightening my top, I resolve to head back to the villa, sort things out with Owen and keep my distance from Leo for the rest of the time he's on this island.

As I climb back up the handful of white stairs leading to the deck, preparing to make my excuses, the engine fires up and the boat starts moving. I've missed my chance to escape.

Now I'm trapped on this boat for the next few hours with my ex-lover and his new girlfriend.

Chapter Eleven
Owen

It's early afternoon and Sienna still hasn't returned to the villa. I've been pacing round and round the enormous house, not wanting to leave in case she comes back and I miss her. I tried calling her mobile, but she's not really been using it here and I followed the sound to her bedside drawer. She likes to completely disconnect while she's on the island. Until now, we've been at each other's side so it hasn't been an issue. But now I'm starting to worry.

Checking my watch, I note that another twenty minutes has slid by. Where is she? Surely she must have finished the speedboat ride with Leo by now? I make my way back through the living room area, where a huge L-shaped white sofa and several white armchairs are gathered around a humongous TV unit. There's a big fan on the ceiling above. From the window, the sandy white beaches are visible. The room is impressive, but it's got nothing on the next part of the house.

I go through the white archway into another expansive room that feels even bigger than it actually is, because one side opens up completely to an outdoor area. There are several white curtains, tied back onto and hiding the stone pillars supporting the structure of the room, but the effect takes my breath away every time I step in the room.

Most of my life has been spent in small, cramped spaces. I reflect on the claustrophobic flats I lived in when I was growing up, followed by the dark and dank bedsits I frequented when I started working in big cities. It's bizarre to think of all of those people back home, huddled together in poorly lit rooms, when places like this exist. For me, this is practically heaven on Earth and such a stark contrast to everything that has come before.

This room contains a pool table, an old-school pinball machine and a tennis table. Directly outside, there's a sturdy wooden structure with a roof made of thatched palm leaves that creates a sheltered area just outside the villa. Within this is a bar stocked with about ten different types of Caribbean rum. And beyond that, under a white gazebo structure, is a hot tub. Needless to say, this is the part of the building where I like to spend most of my time.

Sitting down on a bar stool, I contemplate pouring myself a drink but then decide against it. If Sienna came back and saw me consuming more alcohol that might not go down well. I'm not sure where she got the notion I'm some sort of secret alcoholic. I've never done anything to give her that impression in all the time we've known each other. Then again, everything between us is still new. Perhaps it was just a leap of fear that she made when she saw me behaving like such a wreck last night. Everything I said was true though, I'm not a big drinker so what we had last night knocked me sideways. It didn't help that Leo kept pushing those shots in my direction. They may have been small, but they were lethal.

Padding through the house once more, I try to stop obsessing over Leo and the fact he is probably still with my wife at this very moment. My feet take me back to the bedroom Sienna and I share. I stand on the adjacent balcony, scanning the routes to and from the villa. But there's no sign of her whatsoever.

My patience is starting to wear thin now. So I got drunk. I can't believe Sienna is punishing me for it, when she agreed to have drinks with the other couple in the first place. I didn't even want to socialise with them, I could tell immediately they weren't the sort of people I'd have anything in common with. And I was right.

Hazel is so stuck-up it was painful having a conversation with her. Although I'd take that option any day over Leo's behaviour. He was being territorial with Sienna; he may as well have had a neon sign over his head flashing the words 'alpha male'. I get that, as an employee of her father, he may not want to be too friendly with me. It was more than that though, the way he was being with her wasn't acceptable.

I flip back through the interactions last night: his hand on her knee, draping his arm around her chair and then isolating her for a private chat. It wasn't me being paranoid or overprotective, he was crossing a line. He's a clever guy, that much is obvious, so I'm certain he knew what he was doing.

What I don't know is why. Sienna said Leo worked for her father, she didn't indicate he was also a family friend or even that they knew each other as acquaintances. The chemistry between them suggested something very different. If they have a history together, that's not exactly music to my ears, but if it's in the past I'd rather Sienna just be upfront with me. If she's not being open about her relationship with Leo that suggests there's something she wants to hide.

I don't want there to be secrets in our marriage. Even though I have truths from my own past I need to tell Sienna about, before it's too late.

The clock in the hallway sounds to me as though its ticking louder and louder. I've had enough. I grab my cap and march out of the house. As I turn right out by the wall that runs around the property, I collide smack bang into something solid.

'Looking for someone?'

'Not you again!' I lose my cool when I see Jed's belligerent face mocking me once more.

I storm off without a backward look, seething with frustration. I don't understand why Jed is trying to ruffle my feathers. We weren't exactly friends before, but we got on well enough to pass the time together. I can only assume he's jealous of how things have worked out for me.

After scouring the island, I head down towards the jetty. If they're out on a speedboat that's where they'd be coming back to. It doesn't take me long to get down there to find the speedboat is moored up with no sign of anyone in it.

That's unexpected. I thought maybe they were still out at sea. Or they'd come back and were enjoying a few drinks on the boat.

Then I wonder... the person who told me Sienna was out on a speedboat with Leo was Jed. Maybe he was lying? Perhaps he made it up to play on my emotions. I growl under my breath. I contemplate racing back to the house and confronting Jed. But that's exactly what he wants and, if I do that, he'll know he's got to me. And I don't want to give him the satisfaction.

Sitting down on the jetty, I dip my feet into the water. Straight away, I regret it. The cuts on the foot I hurt this morning sting instantly from the salt in the sea. I curse. My day really couldn't get any worse... or could it?

I try to relax, to tell myself that I'm getting worked up over nothing. I lean back, appreciating the warmth on my face and the sun in the clear blue sky. I'm aware of the frustration still bubbling up inside me. If I could just see Sienna and sort things out, things could go back to normal between us.

The sound of the waves rolling back and forth in a regular rhythm helps to calm my anger. But then I begin to worry that something has happened to Sienna. Maybe she's hurt? Perhaps she needs my help?

'Hey.'

The voice startles me from my thoughts. I see Hazel standing over me and she doesn't seem happy. I stay where I am, not wanting to get too drawn in by this woman. Ever since the other couple arrived on the island yesterday, things have been going wrong between me and Sienna. I just want to get rid of them both as fast as I can.

'Listen, I don't know what kind of game *your wife* is playing at but—'

'Hang on, you've seen Sienna?' I pull myself to standing, now fully alert.

'That's the problem,' Hazel says. 'I've seen a bit too much of Sienna in the last twenty-four hours and so has my boyfriend.'

'What do you mean by that?' My hackles are rising now.

'Your precious Sienna was shamelessly flirting with Leo all morning.'

'This morning? Where?'

'We went out on the speedboat.'

Ah, so Jed hadn't been lying.

'Flirting?'

'Yes, whispering together in corners, pressing up against each other every chance they got.'

My mouth hangs open. Hazel is confirming my worst fears.

'What are you going to do about it?' Hazel hisses.

'Me?' I'm still absorbing the information the woman I recently married has just spent the morning draped over another guy.

Hazel's green eyes flicker in annoyance.

'Maybe they were just being friendly,' I say weakly.

'You and I both know that's not true,' Hazel replies in exasperation. 'You saw how they were last night as well.'

I'm about to respond but Hazel's mobile phone starts ringing. 'Just do something about it,' she says to me through gritted teeth before leaving.

The possibility of losing Sienna to Leo hits me in full force.

I love Sienna with all my heart. She's the best thing that's ever happened to me.

I'm not about to let a guy like Leo take her from me.

If he tries to break us apart, I'll kill him...

Chapter Twelve
Sienna

'Sienna! Thank God you're okay!' Owen's handsome face is creased with concern. 'I was worried sick about you.'

I feel so bad. I only meant to go for a quick walk to clear my head this morning. Somehow Leo pulled me off track. Firstly, with the speedboat ride. I was worried he was going to try to drag me back into a conversation about our past or that he'd say something inappropriate in front of Hazel. I was on edge the whole time but, to my relief, Leo didn't mention our relationship again. Hazel and I sat together sunbathing while Leo, Joseph and Bruce messed about with various speeds and gadgets on the boat. Despite Hazel's haughty demeanour, we managed to find enough to chat about and she seemed to thaw a little. The considered way in which she spoke made me wonder if her high-maintenance appearance was a mask for shyness. I still can't quite understand how she managed to get Leo, the eternal bachelor, to commit and go on a vacation with her but I decided not to probe too much. After all, I'm married now and what Leo does is none of my concern.

As the boat was being steered back to the jetty, Leo started talking business. He was asking questions about potential renovation work and I couldn't stand the thought of some of the suggestions he was making. So I decided to show him myself why his proposals wouldn't work and took him to various locations on the island, with Hazel trailing along with us. I got so caught up in it all that I completely lost track of time. But the island means so much to me, and I don't want Leo and my father to crash in and change the peaceful nature of this place.

Now it's mid-afternoon and I've been away from Owen for hours. It's probably the longest we've been apart since we got married. It's not like we need to be glued to each other's sides but I just wish we hadn't parted on bad words this morning. I hope he doesn't think that I'm still holding a grudge against him.

I rush into his open arms. 'Owen, I'm so sorry.'

His whole body stiffens at my words.

I let out a little sob, my pent-up emotions getting the better of me. 'I'm sorry I've been gone for so long. And I was being ridiculous earlier, can we just forget about it all and have a nice afternoon together?'

'Sienna...' Owen says quietly, but then stops. 'Let's just enjoy the rest of the day.'

'I missed you,' I tell him truthfully.

'Really?' He seems relieved and that makes me feel even more guilty about the way I spoke to him when he woke up this morning. And for taking such a long time to return to the villa.

We embrace again, and I hold him to me a little tighter this time.

'What have you got there?' Owen asks, gesturing to my hands.

'A fresh mango for you.' I hand over the fruit. 'As a peace offering.'

'Accepted.'

I slide my hand into his and we walk around the pool area outside the villa. He bites into the mango and we walk in companionable silence.

'Fancy a swim?' Owen asks, as he finishes eating.

'No, I'm feeling quite tired.'

'Let's just chill with a movie then.'

'Sounds perfect.'

We do just that. Owen brings me a glass of Molly's homemade lemonade and we flick through the channels, chatting about which movie to select. Sometimes I think half the enjoyment is in the choosing of the show or film. I take the opportunity to check my mobile while we're at the villa. I have a number of missed calls from Owen's phone this morning. This makes me feel even guiltier about not coming back to the villa sooner. I also have a dozen missed calls from my father and several messages asking me to ring him back. I wish I hadn't checked the phone now as I don't relish the idea of having to speak with him today. So I switch the device off again and decide to respond tomorrow instead. One day won't make any difference.

I stretch out on the comfortable sofa, feeling tired after being in the sun for too long today. My head is in Owen's lap and he gently strokes my hair. The movie we've chosen is only just beginning but my eyes are already feeling heavy and, before I know it, I'm drifting off to sleep.

***

I lurch awake, my scrambled brain trying to remember my surroundings. A light, white blanket is covering me and I'm on the living room sofa. I sit up and note that the sun is now going down. I must have been asleep for a few hours. I feel disorientated in the way you do when you've unexpectedly fallen asleep during daylight hours.

I stand up too quickly and the room spins a little. I take a second to steady myself. And then I see something that makes me jump with fright. There's a figure sitting on the low wall outside. I thought I was alone and it's so shadowy I'm not sure who it is.

'Hello?' I call. 'Owen, is that you?'

I realise I'm trembling all over. I don't know why I feel so spooked. I usually feel incredibly safe on Oyster Island.

'Owen?' I try again, apprehension loaded in my voice. And then I voice my next guess. 'Leo?'

The figure stands up and starts to come towards me. I realise it's ridiculous for me to be standing here in a darkened room. I manage to reach the light and snap it on. The whole room is lit up and I'm dazzled for a second. Then I see who it is.

It's Owen.

I exhale. 'You frightened me!' My voice is still shaky.

'Why did you call out Leo's name?' Owen asks, a serious expression on his face.

'I called out your name first,' I say slowly. 'I'd only just woken up. I couldn't make out who was sitting outside. I was scared.'

I'm still not entirely awake. I feel groggy and off-kilter.

'But you thought it might be Leo?'

'I didn't know who it was. I'm so glad it was you, Owen.' I feel chilly in the evening breeze and I just want this day to be over now.

I'd like to crawl into my bed and sleep for a good eight hours, to blot out everything and start afresh tomorrow.

'Leo isn't just your father's employee, is he?' Owen says suddenly.

The question hits me out of nowhere. I feel ambushed, like Owen has pounced on me when he can see I'm not functioning properly.

'Owen, Leo is my father's employee. He has an important role and, because of that, he's a family friend.' Everything I've said is true, I just haven't told him the whole truth.

'Sienna, you would tell me if there's something wrong, wouldn't you?'

'Sit down,' I say, pulling Owen back onto the sofa with me. I cup his face in my hands. 'Owen Turner, I married you because I love you and I want to spend the rest of my life with you.'

I kiss him on the lips. 'You've got nothing to worry about where Leo is concerned. You're my husband.'

He kisses me back. I hope this is the end of this conversation. For good.

'I love you Sienna,' Owen whispers gently.

'I love you too Leo.'

As soon as the words are out of my mouth, I realise my mistake. My heart plummets. It's because Leo said those three words to me earlier on today. It's been on my mind ever since.

Owen jerks away from me.

'Leo!'

'Owen! Owen! I'm half asleep!'

Owen looks crestfallen and I just want to wipe the last five minutes and start again. This is not how I wanted to start our married life. We're meant to be on our honeymoon.

'Please Owen—'

'I just need some space,' he tells me. He looks so downcast that my heart squeezes. I can't believe what I've just done.

Owen pads out of the room. This wasn't supposed to be happening. Our honeymoon should be about creating precious memories, instead we've had a day of arguments.

A tear rolls down my cheek but I brush it away quickly.

I know I've hurt him. I need to find a way to convince him that Leo isn't competition. And I need to make sure he doesn't find out about the history between me and Leo. I feel like it would devastate him and there's no reason for him to know. The present is what matters and our marriage vows.

I repeat our promise to each other over and over in my mind, conjuring up the happy day when we exchanged the words I hope we will live by.

For richer, for poorer.

In sickness and in health.

To love and to cherish.

Till death do us part.

Chapter Thirteen
The Killer

Just look at her.

Little. Miss. Perfect.

If I hated her before, I hate her even more now. Everything that's happened on the island has only reinforced my decision.

She has to die.

Watching her there, asleep on the sofa, I know I could get rid of her so very easily. All it would take is a small 'accident' while she's sleeping and it would be done.

But it's not the right time. I need to be patient. I know security is in the room just down the hall and, as much as I want to act now, I can't risk her waking up and alerting them. I want her dead, but I want to get away with it.

After all, I've waited this long. What will one more day hurt? And then she'll be gone.

Forever.

Chapter Fourteen
Owen

Hearing Sienna say the words 'I love you too Leo' was like a dagger to my heart. I know I'm probably overreacting. I know she was tired. I could've just laughed off her calling me another man's name but I'm not good at hiding my true feelings.

She said she didn't mean it. She said it was a mistake. But should I believe her? Or was it a slip of the tongue that revealed more of her true feelings than she intended?

My brain feels too full of conflicting thoughts. Until last night, I thought I could trust Sienna. But now I'm not so sure. It's strange what a difference twenty-four hours can make.

I leave the villa and head past a row of palm trees that all have pretty fairy lights wrapped around their trunks. I smile, despite myself; they have Sienna's taste written all over them. That one fleeting thought brings me back to reality.

As beautiful as this island is, I know the isolation here can give you cabin fever after a while. Being in one place for a long time, without a change of scenery or pace, is tough. The peace and tranquillity here is blissful in lots of ways. Except, the silence and lack of distraction forces you to turn inwards, to examine your own mind, sift through your memories... and focus on your fears.

Not long after I started here, I remember another member of staff, Poppy, telling me the story of a chef who'd worked on the island and had a major breakdown. It wasn't clear whether she knew the poor guy personally or if it was the kind of cautionary tale handed along the line from one employee to another. Poppy herself had worked on the island for five years, with only a handful of returns to the UK.

I asked her what her secret to embracing the island was. And how she stopped herself from spiralling when the isolation became overwhelming.

Her response was clear. Life was way better here than it had been for her back in England, where she'd worked more hours for less pay, less holiday and no chance of living anywhere remotely pretty. So she clung onto the positives, stayed grateful for all the opportunities working here gave her and tried to keep busy.

It was good advice and I need to try and implement it. Because I don't want this to be the beginning of a slippery slope for me. I don't want to end up like that poor chef.

My feet are taking me along the familiar, well-trodden path leading me to the staff quarters. When I was employed here things were very different but I had a place to call my own, my own belongings, my own sense of purpose. It's been strange not to have any of those things recently. I've been feeling like a guest living in someone else's house.

I should share this with Sienna. Maybe there's a room I can claim as my own, or somewhere on the island where I can create something that's just mine. I'd love to have my own patch of earth so I can continue gardening. It's my passion, my hobby, my therapy and my exercise. Not being outdoors, with my hands in the earth and my mind relaxed as I engage in my work, has been very different for me. It's only now I identify how much I've been missing it.

We all have our own ways of coping and our own passions that shape us. Falling in love with Sienna has been such a whirlwind and I wouldn't change it for the world. But I also need to make sure that I'm not uprooting myself so much that I no longer recognise who I am.

With this in mind, I keep walking towards the staff accommodation. I feel awkward having returned to the island and jumped to the other side of the payroll. More than that, I feel rude not having come to say hello to everyone and putting over my side of the story. After all, those people were my friends, acquaintances, colleagues, the people I spent my time with. Perhaps Jed does have a good reason to be annoyed at me.

It will be nice to have a chat with some familiar faces as well. I've never spent as much time with one person in my adult life as I have done with Sienna in these past few months. Perhaps we just need some time out from each other.

I weave through the orchard where a multitude of different fruits are growing; there's everything from lemon and banana trees to coconut and papaya trees. I enjoyed tending this area of the island in particular. Part of the reason why I was drawn to the orchard was because it presented a fresh challenge to get to know new plants that were very different to the ones I used to back in England. Instead, I got even more of a challenge in marrying into the Barker-Jones family.

The smell of oranges sweetens the air around me as I pluck a ripe starfruit from a low-hanging branch. I wonder who has replaced me on the gardening team. Ted, another old-time employee for the Barker-Jones family who had been transferred out here with Molly and Joseph for their golden years, was the head gardener. Alongside him were two very knowledgeable Jamaican guys and then a number of locals employed from nearby islands, including Haiti and Puerto Rico. We all worked well together. And I can't help but imagine what they must think of me now. Perhaps an opportunist or a Romeo? Nothing could be further from the truth, but I'm sure that other people won't see my recent marriage the way I do.

There's a heavy feeling in the pit of my stomach. Sienna and I were never going to be a normal couple on our honeymoon, not given who she is but, even though emotions have been very intense between us, we've been blissfully happy. It's taken the other couple on holiday showing up to cause an argument between Sienna and me. I guess our first falling-out was going to happen at some point. You can't spend every waking second with one person and not end up having disagreements from time to time. But Leo's presence has made me feel uneasy for so many reasons.

He's a good-looking guy, I can see that. He's well regarded by Derek and a successful businessman by all accounts. The thing that bothers me most is the clear chemistry between Sienna and Leo. They know each other much better than Sienna is letting on, but I wonder just how well.

A vision of Leo kissing my wife creeps into my head, and I quickly squash it down. I'm not normally a jealous type but Sienna means everything to me. I push past the last few trees in the orchard and come to the clifftops near the outskirts of the employee apartments. One of the first things you're told when you come to work here is to stick to the paths after nightfall. A wrong turn along this route could result in someone plunging to the inky depths of the sea below when the tide is in, or worse, falling against the jagged and unforgiving rock face when the tide is out.

By now, I'm confident I know the layout of this landscape well enough. So I ignore the warning advice given to me as I stand on the cliff edge, watching the sun set. The sky is a deep burnt orange and it feels as though the world around me is on fire.

I carry on walking for a few more minutes, the light rapidly fading with each step I take. Then, up ahead, I see the outline of a slim, familiar woman silhouetted by the last light of the day. I exhale. It's Sienna. Perhaps she came looking for me.

She's leaning her willowy frame against a tree, her straight hair ruffled in the evening breeze. I stay quiet and move towards her silently. My body being pulled towards her like a magnet, the attraction I feel when she's near me is palpable.

'Sienna,' I breathe, wrapping one arm around her waist from behind and bending slightly to kiss her on the neck.

A scream cuts through the silent night. In that split second, I realise my error.

I spring back.

'Sienna?' I question.

The woman whips around and looks at me with big, wide eyes. I can see she's frightened.

'I'm sorry,' I say, hurriedly backing away. 'I'm sorry, I thought you were someone else...'

She's frozen to the spot. In the dusky evening light, I can see how I mistook her for my wife. This woman could be Sienna's double. Her hair is the same shade of honey-blonde, her height and figure are almost identical. But I realise now that she's a few years younger and, once she's turned towards me, I can see facially she looks very different. Her nose is longer, her cheekbones higher, her mouth fuller. Taking her in, I kick myself for not recognising this woman is wearing a dress and not the t-shirt and shorts Sienna has been in all day.

'Look, it was an honest mistake. Please accept my apology.'

The woman is shivering in the cool evening air.

'What's your name?' I ask.

'Astrid,' she tells me hesitantly.

'Astrid, I genuinely thought you were someone else.' I now vaguely remember her name. I think she's one of the cleaners who works with Molly.

She seems to shake herself down and I hope she is recovering quickly. 'I didn't mean to frighten you. But… could we keep this to ourselves?'

Astrid blinks rapidly, she obviously wasn't expecting me to say that. And I wasn't expecting to ask either. Except, it's now dawning on me that this situation could be very misconstrued. I need to protect myself.

Astrid closes the gap between us and tips her face towards me. 'You mean, keep this a secret?'

I wring my hands, cringing at the way this sounds.

She stands on her toes and whispers in my ear. 'Okay…' And then she kisses me on the lips, a firm kiss loaded with intent.

What the hell is going on? Only a few moments ago I was concerned I'd scared her. Now I'm stunned. I pull away.

'We can keep this a secret,' she smiles slowly at me.

'Astrid, that isn't what I mean.' I'm horrified that she's somehow misinterpreted my meaning. 'I love my wife. I thought you were Sienna. It was a mistake.'

'You and Sienna are all wrong for each other,' Astrid tells me. 'You're from two different worlds. It's never going to work.'

'Excuse me?' I'm feeling angry now. This woman doesn't know me at all and yet she's quite literally pounced on me when she can see I'm confused.

'I've watched you every day since you and Sienna arrived here for your honeymoon. And I've heard the other staff talking about your time working on the island as a gardener. You'd be way more suited to me. We could have something special, something real.'

'What? This is nuts! I don't know you at all.'

'We could change that...'

'Why does no-one seem to understand that I've married my wife because I love her? It doesn't matter who she is or who I am!' I blurt my words out without thinking, my frustration rushing to the surface.

Astrid gives me a pitiful look. 'That's what you think now. Sienna isn't like you or me, though.'

'Look, this was a mistake. And I'm making it very clear there's nothing between us. I'm sorry but I said my marriage vows and I mean to keep them.'

Astrid flutters her long, dark eyelashes. 'It's very sweet of you, but Sienna will break your heart. It's obvious... We could be so good together.'

'Just leave me alone!' I raise my voice more than I intended to.

Astrid blows me a kiss and gives me a small wave goodbye before walking away. I watch her go, my muscles tense. I was worried that she wasn't going to back down so easily.

That was a mad, unexpected encounter. The woman was deluded. Beautiful but deluded. Did she really have feelings for me? Or was she just trying to take advantage of me now my circumstances have changed?

I almost trip over in my rush to put as much distance between myself and Astrid as I can. Except, before I can move away, I hear something that makes my blood run cold. The sound of rustling in the bushes alongside the pathway I'm standing on.

'Is someone there?' I bark out. Has someone just seen me with Astrid? Witnessed her kissing me? Me putting my arm around her?

The sound stops. I should go and investigate. And yet, I'm probably just being paranoid. It's likely to be an animal or the wind ruffling the leaves. I'm just shaken up by the exchange with Astrid.

So I head back to the villa and to my wife.

All the while thinking that maybe coming back to this island wasn't such a good idea after all.

Chapter Fifteen
Sienna

Despite everything that happened yesterday, I feel content and peaceful. A calm settles over me as I fling my arms wide and finish my morning yoga routine. It's a ritual I complete every day, stretching my body as the sun rises. It helps me to de-stress and start the day anew. And I definitely needed it this morning after having my first marital argument yesterday. I still can't believe I said Leo's name instead of Owen's. I don't want to analyse it too closely, I just hope Owen lets it go.

Last night, Owen slipped into bed beside me and we fell asleep in each other's arms. Even though we haven't spoken properly, it seemed as though we were calling a truce with our actions. It felt all wrong to be arguing with him. Today, I intend to do everything I can to show him I'm genuinely sorry and to smooth things over between us. When I go back to the villa, I'm going to ask Molly to whip up one of her delicious, cooked breakfasts for starters. After that, I'll suggest we play a few rounds of table tennis and I might just let Owen win a game too. I'm still pondering plans for this afternoon but spending time in the hot tub and using the sauna could set the tone for a nice, relaxing afternoon.

I make a milky coffee and sip the hot, sweet liquid as I go for a gentle stroll. I can't imagine that anything bad could ever happen, here on this beautiful island, it's so tranquil and I feel so safe here. I just need to disentangle myself from Leo's presence and get back to what's important – making memories on my honeymoon with my gorgeous new husband.

Each morning, I vary my walk, taking a different route around Oyster Island. Yesterday, I meandered down to one of the beaches and allowed my toes to sink into the soft, inviting sand. I surveyed the clear blue sea and listened to the birds twittering in the treetops. Today, my feet take me in a completely different direction. I skirt round the edges of the whitewashed villa, and along the winding path that leads to the high clifftop on the north side of the island.

I skirt along the edges of the clifftop, every so often daring myself to look at the vast drop below. The sky is awash with beautiful deep pinks, purples and oranges. The turquoise sea contrasts beautifully and it's like I'm looking at a painting. There's a slight breeze in the air and I enjoy the feel of the wind rippling in my hair as I watch a small fishing boat bobbing in the water. I sigh deeply, embracing the day.

As I move, the tension in my muscles loosens and the worries of yesterday start to disappear. I manage to cover a fair distance and find myself nearing the section of the cliff that gives way to natural steps leading down to an idyllic lagoon. It was the place Owen and I went to on the second night of our honeymoon, just under a week ago. A smile plays across my lips as I remember our romantic evening together by the sea, under the stars.

Straying to the top of the steps, I look down, wondering whether I have time to descend and take a dip in the ocean before my husband wakes up. But the thought goes straight from my mind as I gaze down the steep, stony staircase and see a red trail of blood.

I freeze, panicked by the sight. It's not just a few blood spots, there's a lot of dark, red blood.

Perhaps an animal has been hurt? Or maybe someone is in trouble?

I take a deep breath, not really wanting to look again but knowing I'd never forgive myself for turning away if I could help in some way.

Standing on the first step, I look down at the dizzying drop below. My nails are digging hard into the palms of my hands. I can't see anything, so I take another step, and then another until I'm part way down the twisting route to the lagoon.

And then I see it.

A woman's body, crumpled at the foot of the steps. The neck at an unnatural angle.

No-one could survive a fall like that.

Her honey-blonde hair is fanned out around her. Her slim figure is broken beyond repair. I recognise her the newest member of staff. What a devastating way for her young life to end.

Did she slip and fall? Was this an accident? Or did someone push her? Was this deliberate?

Looking at the craggy side of the cliff, I feel sick as I spot a fragment of material snagged on a rock. The distinctive, bright fuchsia colour matches the dress the woman at the bottom of the steps is clothed in. It seems clear she fell from the top of the cliff and down onto the latter half of the natural staircase cut into the cliff-face, before landing at the bottom of the final sandy step.

A sob rises inside of me as I think of her poor body falling down the unforgiving descent before finally coming to a stop. Such a tragic and brutal way to die.

I turn around, wanting to put some distance between me and the dead woman, knowing I need to report what I've seen straight away. Instead, I'm shocked to see a man now standing on the top step looking down at me. There's a grimace across his face and he has a piece of the fuchsia material in his hand.

My heart hammers in my chest and I fight to keep my balance and stay upright. I don't feel reassured by his presence, I feel frightened.

Am I next?

That's the thought that enters my mind first as I look between the unmoving woman below and the man towering above me. Despite the fact I know every line of his face so well. Despite the fact that he shouldn't be a threat to me. His expression is unrecognisable and I have no idea why he is here.

My heart is thudding against my ribcage.

Can I trust him?

Or am I about to die too?

Chapter Sixteen
Owen

Sienna isn't in the bed when I wake. This isn't unusual, she's an earlier riser and I'm not. I still find it strange that I don't have to drag myself out of bed every morning to go to work. Don't get me wrong, I loved my job as a gardener, but I didn't love having to get up at 6.30 a.m. every morning.

Nowadays, I can find a more natural rhythm for my body. While we were in Cuba together, at the start of our month there, I made an effort to get up at the same time Sienna did. But, very quickly, we slipped into the routine of Sienna going off to do her yoga workout first thing and me getting a little bit more beauty sleep.

It's good for Sienna to have time to herself in the day, and I need to do the same thing. Carve out some space to focus on something purposeful. I don't fancy yoga but I would like to be more consistent with my weight training. Since we've been here, I've done a few sessions in the gym that's in a small outbuilding in the grounds of the villa but I should be doing more, especially now I'm not getting all the outdoor exercise that I've previously been used to.

It's only after I've been lying awake for five minutes, listening to the ocean, that the events of yesterday evening come crashing back to me. I groan out loud. I don't know what was worse, my wife saying another man's name instead of mine or Astrid taking advantage of my error and then kissing me.

I need to make sure Astrid doesn't start blabbing to the other staff about what happened. She could exaggerate our encounter. It would be my word against hers. Although, there was something in the way that she looked at me yesterday that suggested she wasn't getting close to me just for the sake of creating gossip. I believe she did have feelings for me, and that could be a much more difficult scenario to navigate. I have to ensure Astrid's not going to do anything to make either of our lives complicated.

Padding into the spacious bathroom I place my hands either side of the sink and pull the situation apart in my mind. Turning on the gold tap, I splash my face with ice-cold water to wake myself up. Catching sight of myself in the mirror, I see that my jaw is tightly clenched and my eyes a little bloodshot. I shake my head, it's no good. I know the best thing to do is to be honest with Sienna. I should tell her what happened with Astrid last night, but the thought of doing so makes my jaw lock even more.

Coming clean would take a weight off my shoulders. It should show Sienna that being transparent is the way in which I want to conduct our marriage, so that we have a foundation built on truth. Perhaps she can then share with me what's really going on between her and Leo. And, in turn, I can share the secrets of my own past with her.

Combing my hair and brushing my teeth, I'm sure that I've hit upon the right course of action. So why do I feel so nervous? Why am I worried about whether or not Sienna will believe me? I've got so much to lose now, and I'd be crushed if Sienna looked at me with mistrust in her eyes.

Changing into a loose vest top and shorts, I resolve that, as well as talking things through with Sienna, I'm going to do some exercise today. It might help to clear my foggy brain. Wandering outside, I see that Sienna isn't in her usual yoga spot, under the custom-built mahogany pergola, so she must have finished already. I assume she's off on her morning stroll so I guess the route she may have taken and amble along, enjoying the morning light.

I make a mental note to speak to Sienna about keeping her mobile phone on her. The island isn't big, but I don't want to keep chasing after her when she goes off in the morning. There are plenty of nooks and crannies across Oyster Island and Sienna knows this place much better than I do.

Without realising it, I find myself treading the same path as last night. I steer left of the orchard and walk nearer to the clifftop, deliberately avoiding the spot where Astrid and I had our encounter last night. I feel uncomfortable as I think about Astrid being so close to me.

The water looks so inviting today, it's fresh and clear. The sweep of the bay gives me a tingle of happiness and I almost have to pinch myself again as I remember just how lucky I am to be here with the love of my life. I just hope my good fortune doesn't start to run out...

I'm almost at the northern tip of the island now. The views from here are stunning. Sienna and I spent the second night of our honeymoon down by a little lagoon in this quiet area. I know it's one of Sienna's favourite spots, so I make my way towards it now. On the ground in front of me, I see a bright patch of colour. Kneeling down, I discover it's a piece of material. It looks like a torn piece of clothing.

I stand up hastily, clutching the piece of cloth in my hand, instantly worried there's something wrong.

As I get to the steps leading down to the lagoon, I realise I'm not the only person here. I see my wife part way down the steps, but something about her posture doesn't look right. And then I look beyond her, to the bottom of the steps.

I see the blood. I see the body.

I'm horrified. And then I see who it is.

It's Astrid.

The woman who confessed she had feelings for me last night. The woman who kissed me. She's dead.

This is a complete disaster. My mouth is set in a grimace and I can feel a deep worry line forming on my forehead. I try to picture Astrid's expression as she turned away from me last night. Did she walk in this direction after she left? And what happened next?

Staring down at the scene, I register Sienna's eyes locking onto mine. She's gone completely white and, for a terrible second, I think she might faint and lose her balance.

'Sienna!' I take the steps two at a time. She recoils back from me slightly. There's something wrong.

I reach out to her but she screams and barges past me, sprinting to the top of the steps.

I follow her and she screams at the top of her voice again.

'Calm down!' I shout at her. 'You need to calm down.'

Oh God. Has Sienna done this? Did she find out about me and Astrid? And did she seek her revenge?

'What happened?' I ask, not really believing Sienna has it in her to end someone's life, but I have to find out the order of events.

'I was about to ask you the same thing,' Sienna retorts, her voice more forceful than I was expecting.

'Uh, I only just got here,' I say, feeling ambushed by her question. 'Was she dead when you got here?'

'Yes.' Sienna looks back towards the steps and shudders.

'Are you okay?' I try to step closer to her.

'Of course I'm not okay!' Sienna shouts at me and starts to move backwards, increasing the space between us but still keeping her eyes firmly on me.

'Where are you going?'

Sienna stops in her tracks. 'I have to get away!'

'Sienna, what's going on?'

'Why were you here, Owen?' Her lower lip trembles as she speaks.

'I came to find you.'

'Why here?'

'I didn't come here straight away, I've been wandering. I knew this spot was a favourite of yours.'

'Did you see what happened to Astrid?' I keep my voice as measured and level as I can.

'How do you know her name?' Sienna questions, a look of pure fear on her face.

'She's a member of staff,' I say in a rush, cursing myself for slipping up and revealing a connection.

'Did you hurt her?'

'What? No! Sienna, how can you say that?'

'I need to get my security, it's not safe here any more.'

'Well let me come with you, I want you to be safe. I want to look after you.'

'I have to follow my security protocol.'

I know how scary this situation must be for her. She's told me about previous security breaches, but none of them have been on Oyster Island. So I try not to lose my patience, however frustrated I am by her reaction.

'Let's get you to Bruce and...'

'No! I need go alone.'

Logically, I'm aware her security training has drilled this mindset into her. But I'm her husband, she can't really think I've got anything to do with this, can she?

'Sienna, don't you trust me?'

She doesn't answer and her silence speaks volumes. I'm astonished at how quickly she's jumping to conclusions.

'How well do we really know each other?'

Her question hangs in the air. I didn't think that mattered, I thought we got each other, there was a spark between us. But how many people have pressed that question upon Sienna? How many people have asked her if she really knows me that well? Her father. Her mother. Leo. Molly even?

'You know me, Sienna,' I say quietly.

She pulls at her hair, looking tormented. 'Owen, what the hell is going on?'

'Sienna, all I know is what I saw right now. You, standing on the steps. And Astrid, dead at the bottom of them.'

'Are you saying you think I did it?' Sienna shrieks.

Worried I've said the wrong thing, I answer in a desperate rush. 'No Sienna. I know you'd never harm anyone. I'm just pointing out that it's ridiculous to be accusing one another.'

Her face clears and I think she's going to come down from her initial hysterical reaction but then emotion gets the better of her and tears begin cascading down her face.

'Sweetheart, come here,' I say gently.

But she doesn't. She goes in the opposite direction. Away from me.

And I wonder if this is the moment that I've lost her.

Chapter Seventeen
Sienna

My legs burn as I push myself to go as fast as I can, back towards the villa. I fumble in my pocket but my mobile isn't there. I forget to carry it with me when I'm on the island. As I'm running, a jumble of thoughts race through my mind. I berate myself for my stubborn refusal to carry a panic button with me on Oyster Island. Bruce tried to persuade me again when we arrived here last week but I was so set on feeling free.

'Bruce! Kostas!' I shout into the distance, hoping one of my security guards might be miraculously nearby, even though I know it's unlikely. The morning is young and most people will still be having breakfast.

The tears continue to flow down my cheeks. All I can think of is that poor woman's body, crumpled at the bottom of the cliff. I've never seen a dead body before and I wasn't expecting to come across one this morning. The whole incident has shaken me up in a way I've never experienced before.

I hear something crunch behind me and I swivel my head to check over my shoulder. I've been running full pelt without slowing down. I expect to see Owen following me, but there's no-one there. This unnerves me all the more because I'm sure I heard something – or someone.

Adrenalin courses through my body, spurring me on, back towards the villa. I'm longing to see the bulky shapes of Bruce and Kostas. Anywhere else in the world, they're my shadows, my protectors. It's only on Oyster Island I roam free, because I feel truly safe here. Until now...

I hear the noise again. It sounds like a twig snapping under someone's foot. I check over my shoulder once more, but again there's no-one there. My cheeks burn as I think about how I spoke to my husband; how quick I was to point the finger of blame at him. I was too hasty, I know that. But my primal instincts kicked in and the need to protect myself was my overriding driver. Seeing Owen there, in the same vicinity as the body, with the torn piece of fuchsia dress in his hand, made me question everything.

I know it makes me selfish to put myself first but it's the way I've been taught to think. My parents have always instilled in me the knowledge that I could be a target for an abduction or someone seeking revenge, because not everybody likes the businesses my father runs. And, like all TV and newspaper distributions, there's always a political leaning to them. My father has forged alliances with people in power, he's chosen who to support, who to back, and who to take payoffs from. He's created plenty of enemies in his time and that's why I've always been so protected.

My whole life has been like living in a fragile bubble, and I'm hyper aware it could burst loudly and dramatically as a result of decisions and actions that have absolutely nothing to do with me. I could be caught in the middle of a power struggle. I always have that fear hanging over me. Thankfully, I've only experienced a handful of security breaches but they've been terrifying enough that I never want to go through anything like that ever again. A couple of them happened when I was much younger and have scarred me for life, so it's no wonder I'm so paranoid.

So yes I'm hysterical and I'm viewing everything around me as a potential threat. But that's because I'm genuinely afraid. There could be a killer loose on the island. And it's very possible that I'm their target. Because the similarities between the woman at the bottom of the cliff and me didn't escape my notice. Her blonde hair, her fair skin, her similar height. All of those things have made me a hundred times more frightened, because it's very possible that someone has done this as a warning. Or worse. They meant for it to be me.

My lungs are heaving and I have to slow down, but I'm not too far now. Safety is in sight, the villa is around the next bend, just past the guest accommodation and the row of palm trees. My head is pounding and I'm focused on getting to the villa and alerting my security guards. But, out the corner of my eye, I see the wooden door to the biggest guesthouse opening. Leo is standing in the doorframe. I don't know what makes me do it, but I veer off course and run straight to him. Straight into his open arms.

'You have to help me!' I cry, sobbing into his shoulder.

'Come in.' Leo's voice is all concern. 'What's going on?'

'I don't know, I don't know...' My voice is high-pitched and strained.

'Sit down.' Leo guides me inside to a comfortable armchair and I sink into it, my whole body aching.

'Is anyone else here?' I scan the room around me, but I can't see any sign of Hazel or any of the staff.

'No, it's only me. You're shaking, what's happened to you?' Leo persists. 'Has someone hurt you?'

'No...' My voice wobbles. 'But someone might be trying to.' I burst into fresh tears and Leo's face creases.

'Sienna, talk to me.'

I try to start explaining but my voice is croaky with emotion.

Leo kneels down in front of me, he tucks a strand of my blonde hair behind my ear. 'Let me get you a drink of water and you can start at the beginning.'

I hadn't realised how thirsty I was, my throat is red raw after I screamed at Owen. I nod in acceptance.

'Don't worry, you're safe here with me,' Leo says softly before he goes out of the room.

Settling back in the vintage teak armchair and closing my eyes, I inhale deeply. Absorbing the scent of the aged leather fabric of the chair, I try and regain a bit more control of myself. My instinct tells me that Astrid didn't go over the edge of that cliff by accident. I think she was killed.

That means that someone is responsible. And I'm trapped on the island with a killer.

Why did I run to Leo? Why did I feel safe coming to him and not to Owen?

Owen has never shown me anything but love and yet I have my father's voice echoing in my ears, telling me I barely know him. And the whisper of my mother's view that he's just a common gardener, and I know nothing of his background.

Am I starting to regret my hasty marriage? Should I have been more sensible?

Everything feels so right when it's just me and Owen together. But finding a dead body on my precious island has thrown my emotions up in the air. Leo may be the ex who didn't commit when I was in love with him but I've known him since I was a teenager. We have so many shared experiences and, when I saw him standing in the doorway, he represented a known quantity in a way that Owen can't compete with.

My eyes fly open when I hear a sound but it's only Leo coming back in with a glass of water. I accept it and drink my fill. I notice Leo has pulled on a light, casual sweatshirt, in contrast to the sleek, trendy outfits he usually wears, and it alters his appearance. Somehow, he seems younger and more boyish this morning, the sweatshirt reminding me of weekends we spent holed up in his city flat. I try to dislodge the thought, knowing Leo's words yesterday have had an effect on me but feeling terrible for dwelling on thoughts of our past.

In an attempt to distract myself from wandering down a black hole of 'what ifs?' alongside my fears about what Astrid's death could signify, I try and focus on my surroundings. I don't often come to the guesthouses and I'd forgotten how sumptuous this one, the largest of the three, is. As well as being the biggest of the guesthouses it's also the oldest and a little more formal in feel. The main villa has lots of white and neutral tones whereas the interior of this house has dark wooden furniture and plenty of big, leafy green plants set against lighter walls and wooden floors. The windows have enormous shutters and there are a number of colourful pieces of artwork, sourced from various islands across the Caribbean, hanging around the property.

'So, are you going to tell me what's going on?' Leo grabs a stool and sits in front of me, taking my hand in his, and pulling my attention back to the current circumstances.

I gulp in a lungful of air. 'I went for a walk and... down by the lagoon. There's a dead body.'

Leo sits up straight. 'A body?'

'Yes, it's one of the staff... it was awful...' I can't help myself, I begin to sob again, the image of poor Astrid coming into my mind again.

'Hey,' Leo says, moving closer and putting an arm around me.

'I just can't believe it.' I bury my head in his shoulder, glad of his reassuring presence.

'I'm going to ask this,' Leo says steadily. 'Are you certain that's what you saw?'

'Absolutely,' I reply. 'She was on the bottom step, her neck...'

'Okay, okay,' Leo soothes me, stroking my hair.

'I don't think it was an accident,' I stutter, and I tell him about the fuchsia material snagged on the side of the cliff and the blood on the steps.

'Damn!' Leo exclaims. 'This isn't good.' He stands up and starts to pace the room.

'There's something else,' I add. 'I'm worried. The girl, she had blonde hair, about the same height as me. I'm scared it's some sort of warning... or that it was meant to be me.'

Leo swears and rubs the back of his neck. 'We need to get to the bottom of this quickly. Do you have any idea who she was?'

'Owen told me her name was Astrid.'

'Astrid? And Owen told you that?'

'Yes, he was there. He saw her too.'

'He was with you?' Leo questions.

'Not exactly, he appeared at the same spot a little while after I got there.' I'm not ready to tell Leo that Owen had a piece of the fuchsia dress in his hand.

Leo looks around in confusion, as if expecting Owen to materialise.

'I... we parted ways.'

'Why?'

I hang my head, not wanting to admit this. 'I just got spooked about why he was there.'

Leo comes to sit on the stool in front of me again. 'Sienna, you know we need to let the authorities know what's happened. It's important we alert them in case someone is responsible for Astrid's death.'

Leo pauses and takes my hand once more.

'But before we do, there's something I need to tell you.'

My heart sinks. From his tone, I'm certain it's not information I'm going to want to hear.

'I saw Owen last night.'

I want to cover my ears and block out this nightmare but I remain seated, waiting to find out what Leo has to say.

'I saw Owen and Astrid together.'

'What do you mean... together?'

'They were kissing.'

I gasp. It feels like the world has turned on its axis. This can't be true, can it?

'Leo, are you certain?'

'I saw with my own eyes. Astrid, she is – she was – the cleaner for this house. She introduced herself to me and Hazel when we first arrived and I've seen her once since then as well. So I know it was her. And... I'm sorry Sienna, but I have no doubt it was Owen either.'

I'm taken aback by what Leo has just told me. Surely it's not true? Owen seemed completely devoted to me, I would never have expected him to cheat. I thought he cared for me.

'He walked up to her, put one arm around her waist and kissed her neck.' Leo goes on.

'No!' I feel light-headed. 'I don't want to hear it.'

'I think it's best if you do, because there's more.'

'Leo, please, I don't need to be tortured with a blow-by-blow account.' This is just awful. My mind is in turmoil. Leo seems so sure of what he's seen and yet it doesn't seem to add up. This doesn't sound like the Owen I know and love.

'Sienna, you need to hear what happened. It's important,' Leo ploughs on and I sit there, with my head in my hands, wishing I could make him stop.

'Astrid then turned around and kissed Owen. He kissed her back. They looked very familiar with one another. I was shocked to see them all over each other but then the mood between them changed very quickly. And I was even more shocked when I saw them arguing. Owen shouted at her.'

My head snaps up. 'He shouted at her?'

'He didn't look too happy. She started walking away, in the direction of the lagoon.'

'Oh my God, what are you saying?'

'I don't know. I didn't stick around to see if Owen followed her. But if they were arguing in that area last night and this morning Astrid has been found at the bottom of the cliff, it doesn't look good for Owen.'

I gasp again. Even though I jumped to conclusions when I was with Owen, only half an hour ago, I was in a blind panic. I was frightened for my safety and everyone else's opinions of Owen were crowding my thoughts. I hoped my assumptions weren't true. But now, if what Leo is saying is true, it could place Owen as one of the last people to speak to Astrid alive.

Was my husband really cheating on me? Why were he and Astrid arguing? And would he really have pushed her to her death?

There's so much I don't know and so many things that don't seem to make any sense. Owen went out last night but it was only for a short while. When he came back, I didn't notice anything out of the ordinary. Yes, we'd argued but he went for a walk and came back. He got into bed with me and put his arm around me. He whispered 'I love you' into my ear. He hadn't been out of the villa for more than an hour. Could he really have had a meeting with a lover during that time? And could he really have killed her too?

It seems so inconceivable to think Owen would have done that. Despite everyone saying I don't know him well enough, I really thought I did. I believed he was my soul mate.

But what if he's a killer?

Chapter Eighteen
Owen

Big, fat droplets of rain are starting to fall. At first, I welcome the cool relief after a week of long, hot days of the sun beating down upon us. The sky is filled with black, angry clouds which are casting a shadow of darkness across everything. It's only mid-morning but outside it looks like it could be the early evening.

My heart feels as though it's cracking in two. Sienna ran from me, like she was frightened, like she thought I had something to do with Astrid's death. I can understand why she reacted in the way she did. Since she was a child, she's had to deal with all kinds of threats to her life because of who her father is. She's been taught to run from dangerous situations. I'm just shocked that she ran from me too. After all, I came upon her standing metres from a dead body, not the other way round. Perhaps it was just her primal reaction to get to a safe place. But my gut instinct is telling me it was more than that. Maybe everyone's doubts about our marriage and the question of whether Sienna, a beautiful woman, the only daughter of one of the world's richest people, can trust the lowly gardener she fell in love with have finally got to her. Or perhaps she somehow already knows about Astrid kissing me...

Everything is so screwed up. I'd made the decision to come clean to Sienna about what happened with Astrid, but how can I do that now? Because admitting I saw Astrid last night, that she came onto me, and that I shouted at her to leave me alone will surely make me prime suspect number one.

This time last week, my life felt like a beautiful dream. Now, it's turning into a hellish nightmare. Sienna has told me about the constant target that she has on her back. But it's only now this is happening that I can even begin to imagine the impact it's had on her life. I've heard her having bad dreams, dreams where she relives the time a woman snatched her in a shopping centre when she was just five years old. Thankfully, the nanny she was with acted swiftly and the centre went into lockdown, containing the kidnapper and saving Sienna, but having to go through something like that at such a young age must have been so scary.

It just goes to show money can't buy you everything and being wealthy can cause all kinds of problems. When Sienna first told me about the shopping centre incident it made me realise what a big deal it was that she'd opened her heart to me. And that she put her faith in me and our relationship.

And now, being confronted with the body of a woman who looks eerily like her... it makes me wonder what kind of unhinged person might be after my wife. So even though our relationship could be hanging in the balance and my innocence could be in question, that's not my first concern. My first concern is Sienna's safety. Because it's very possible there's a murderer amongst us and they intend for Sienna to be next.

As I arrive back to the villa, I search every room trying to locate my wife. She's nowhere to be seen. I dig my mobile phone out of the bottom of my suitcase and switch it on. I don't have any signal, which isn't unusual on this island. It hasn't bothered me too much before, but it's certainly bothering me now. So I head to one of the downstairs rooms, where I know the surveillance cameras operate from and where I'm likely to find one, if not both, of Sienna's bodyguards.

'Bruce! Kostas!' I shout. 'Guys!'

Entering the room, I'm frustrated to see it's empty. There's no sign of either man. Often they're patrolling the island, and it's not like they're tied to staying here. But I'm so used to coming into this room and finding at least one of them with their feet up, chewing on some gum, so it completely throws me to see the place vacant.

I check the pool area and the grounds but there's no sign of anyone. I can feel myself starting to sweat, and it's not just because of the humidity. The rain has stopped briefly now but the sun hasn't broken out. The clouds still hang above me, low and ominous, they seem to be pressing down and trapping the heat all the more.

A dark thought enters my mind. What if Sienna has gone to Leo? I hope this isn't the case, but it seems the next logical place to look. So I take off in the direction of the guesthouses, which are just a stone's throw from the main villa. Leo's is the biggest one, I know this because he went on about how much potential it had when we had drinks. The building is yet another item on Leo's long list of island upgrades.

Banging on the solid wooden door, I call out Leo's name. He opens up pretty fast.

'Owen, to what do I owe the pleasure?'

'Have you seen Sienna?'

Leo shrugs his shoulders, looking nonchalantly at me. 'What if I have?'

'Is she here?' I ask, still trying to keep my breathing steady.

'I'm here.' Sienna appears in the hallway behind Leo. A wave of relief washes over me. She's safe. That's all that matters.

I step forward to gain access to the house.

'Not so fast, buddy,' Leo commands. He pulls the door to and acts as a barrier in the remaining gap. 'I don't think Sienna wants to see you right now.' He seems to be enjoying this, an amused smile playing across his face.

'Sienna can tell me that for herself, can't she?' I growl in a low voice.

'If I was you, I'd step away. You're already in enough hot water as it is.'

'What the hell? I just want to make sure my wife is safe.'

'She is safe... with me.'

'Sienna! Sienna, come and talk to me.' I try to shout past Leo. 'I'm worried about you. I just want to look after you.'

Leo glares at me now. 'I've told you: she doesn't want to see you. End of.'

He goes to close the door fully but I jam my shoulder in before it's too late. And that's when I lose it.

'Just let me in! She's my wife.'

'For now,' Leo says in a low, antagonistic tone.

He gives the door another shove and I'm sent flying backwards. The door clicks cruelly shut. A red mist descends upon me and I shout Sienna's name louder and louder.

There's no response from the occupants inside the house. So I hammer blows upon the heavy, solid door. I know it's fruitless but what else can I do? I can feel Sienna slipping through my fingers. The longer she's with Leo, the less likely I am to ever hold her in my arms again. I can just imagine the potential poison he might be pouring into her ear. I was wary of Leo from the start, and I was right to be.

It's clear Sienna isn't going to come to the door and speak to me. I'm aware I'm making things worse by reacting in this way. So I force myself to stop and, as much as it pains me to walk away from my wife, knowing she's behind those walls with a man who's made it very clear that he doesn't respect me, I realise I have to find another way of approaching this. Before I leave, I shout: 'Leo, you'd better look after her. You'd better make sure she doesn't come to any harm.'

Acting fast is essential. I have no idea what Leo's part in all this is. Sienna could still be in danger without even realising it. She might trust Leo Harrison but I certainly do not. As I stalk away, I begin to form a plan. I need to get to the other side of the island, so I scout out the nearest golf buggy. They're meant to just be for the use of the staff, with Sienna preferring to get about the island on foot and her father insisting they're not a suitable mode of travel for any guests. But I've ridden these small vehicles a ton of times and, given that I can't seem to shake off the label of being a previous member of staff, I may as well take advantage of my knowledge of where they're stored to help me with the plan that's starting to form in my head.

Sienna may not want to speak to me right now. She's probably still completely shaken up and, with Leo at her side, I'm sure she's being told that she should stay away from me. Just in case the working-class Romeo has something to do with the dead body. I can practically hear the way in which Leo is spinning this whole incident to his advantage. When Sienna told him of our wedding, I could see the jealousy written all over him. It's obvious he wants Sienna, and he's not afraid to play dirty to take her from me.

But I'm not so easily beaten. I grew up in the school of hard knocks and I know how to fight back when I need to. And now it seems I'm gearing up for the biggest fight of my life. Leo might be clever, but he will only be thinking of himself whereas I have Sienna's feelings and wellbeing at the forefront of my mind. So I fire up the golf buggy and set off towards the one person on this island who might be able to get Sienna to listen to reasonable advice. One person who I believe cares for her as much as I do.

I rap firmly on the door of the lodge and Joseph Tanner opens it. He swipes his hand over the back of his mouth, wiping away some crumbs.

'All right,' he says, eyeing me suspiciously. 'We were wondering when you might pop down here to say hello to everyone.'

It's ironic that last night I was intending to do exactly that, and that's how all this mess started in the first place.

'We were just having a spot of lunch; do you want to join us?'

'Thanks but no,' I say. The food smells delicious but I can't eat at a time like this, not when there's so much at stake.

'Sit yourself at the table,' Joseph gestures to a circular table in the middle of a decent-sized kitchen. The Tanners obviously got a good deal when the accommodation was being sorted out, and so they should. According to Sienna, they've worked hard all their lives for the Barker-Jones family.

'Hello dearie,' Molly says, her Irish lilt welcoming and comforting. Exactly what I need right now. 'I've got freshly baked bread here.' She puts a plate down in front of me which contains a baguette cut in half and smothered in butter. 'And some tomato soup coming right up.'

'Molly, that's very kind of you but I don't have time for food. This is urgent.' I hover by the table.

'Don't have time for food!' Molly chuckles. 'You youngsters! You've got enough time to mess around on your social media sites and yet you can't spare any time for your basic human needs!'

'I mean it—'

'She always makes more than we need,' Joseph says, patting his rotund stomach and interrupting me.

'You don't understand,' I persist as Molly ladles the piping hot soup into a bowl. I don't have time to waste. Not when Sienna could be in danger.

'It looks like a storm's a-coming,' Joseph observes; he's either not heard me or he's deliberately ignoring me. He peeks out of the window before sitting down. 'So we thought it was a good excuse for something other than a salad.'

'Don't get me wrong,' Molly interjects, 'I like a salad when it's hot but it's nice to have some variety.' She pauses and then says, 'Go on with you, sit down, we won't bite.'

'It's not that. I need your help. It's Sienna. She's—'

'Have you had your first marital row?' Joseph asks immediately, setting his spoon down on the table and looking intrigued.

'No... yes... but that's not what's important now.'

Molly and Joseph share a look.

'Sienna's in danger!' I protest, starting to lose my patience now. I explain everything that's happened so far this morning, from when I woke up, to finding Sienna on the steps, recognising Astrid's body and now Sienna being with Leo.

'Goodness,' Molly wipes a tear from her eye. 'Astrid's gone. She was so young. It just goes to show, you never know when your time is up.' Joseph passes a hanky over to Molly and moves round to pat her back. The couple must have been together thirty years or more and the close bond between them is obvious. That's exactly what I want for me and Sienna, a love that endures. But can we come back from today?

Joseph crosses his arms. 'What is the world coming to... I thought we were safe here...'

'Me too,' agrees Molly, giving a little sniffle. 'Poor, poor girl. She had her troubles, but she didn't deserve to die like that.'

'Do you know of anyone who might want to harm her?' I ask. 'Are there any of the staff who she didn't get on with? Who might have a grudge against her?' I'm trying to gauge if there's anyone who could obviously have a motive for murder.

Molly purses her lips. 'Astrid didn't have the most easy-going nature,' she says carefully. 'But there's no-one in our little community who would go as far as that, even if there had been a disagreement. We pride ourselves on being thorough with our interviews. Yes, the recruitment agency narrows down the applicants, but we're the ones who determine who's a good fit for the team and the island. Besides, she's only worked here for a month.'

Molly puffs out her chest proudly. Her words are intended to reassure me but they end up doing the exact opposite. After all, she hired me and I ended up marrying Sienna. And, more than that, there's things about my past that the Tanners don't know about. Things I managed to hide when I was applying for my job. So they can't be as thorough as they think…

'Well, it's good to hear there are no obvious candidates who would target Astrid. But that makes me even more concerned for Sienna's safety.'

'Why?' Joseph questions. But I can see Molly has already connected the dots.

'Because Astrid looked just like our Sienna.'

'I wouldn't say that…' Joseph starts.

'Not if you know them both well, no. But they're similar in height, colouring… in the dark it would be easy to make that mistake.'

I swallow, because of course that is exactly the error I made myself last night. I mistook Astrid for Sienna, but I kissed her. And that was it.

'Let's go and get her then,' Joseph says, standing up quickly. 'You did right to come to us.'

'Yes, Sienna's like the daughter we never had,' Molly adds, a sad smile on her face. 'I love her like she was my own.'

'And I don't trust that Leo as far as I could throw him.'

'What do you mean?'

'Joseph!' Molly reprimands him. 'You can't say that.'

'I can. He's a slippery fish and I'd rather she wasn't with him meself.'

I'm glad to hear that Joseph holds the same opinion as me.

I just hope we get to Sienna before anything else happens…

Chapter Nineteen
The Killer

It's a shame Astrid is dead. I didn't mean to kill her, but she was in the wrong place at the wrong time.

Everyone knows Sienna's morning routine. Yoga, coffee, a walk alone. All I had to do was wait until she was alone and then...

Unfortunately, I got a little too eager. When I saw a woman standing there in the dull morning light by the edge of that cliff, with her honey hair and slim frame, I saw my chance and took it.

Do I feel guilty? Of course I do. I'm not a monster.

But the one good thing to come out of this is I know for certain I can go through with killing Sienna.

Why?

Because now I've killed once, I know I can do it again.

Chapter Twenty
Sienna

'He's gone.'

Leo doesn't need to tell me this. I heard every word of the exchange between Owen and Leo and I've listened to Owen's fists pounding the door for the last five minutes before going quiet.

When Owen arrived, hearing him outside made me wobble. It reminded me how much I love the sound of his voice and all the dreams I had for our future. He's the man I married; I should have let him in. Yet witnessing him turn so violent so quickly shook me. I've never seen him so angry and, quaking in the hallway while he batters the door, I woke up to the possibility there could be another side to my husband that he's only just starting to reveal.

'Why don't you go and rest in one of the bedrooms, you've had a draining morning and a nasty shock. I'll get some food for you.' Leo guides me upstairs.

'No, I couldn't eat anything.'

'Okay, well while that nutcase has been carrying on out there—'

'Leo, he's still my husband!'

Leo pulls a face. 'I've tried getting through to security and there's no answer. The phone connectivity is low. So I need to go and find them and I'm going to send an alert out via the security room. I'm not taking any chances where your safety is concerned. The police will need to get involved as well. I'm sure Astrid's death is going to result in a murder investigation.'

I step into one of the upstairs rooms and head straight to the window. There's no sign of Owen out there, so he must've given up and left. I feel a little disheartened that he went away so soon. My emotions are all over the place, I don't know what to think or feel. My world feels as though it's been tipped upside down.

'I'm also going to need to inform your father.'

'Oh!' My hands fly to my face. 'Daddy is going to go mental!'

Leo nods gravely. 'We're going to need to try and contain this. If the competition gets hold of this news they'll have a field day. I can see the headlines now. They won't go easy on your father if there's been a murder on his private island.'

I bite my lip. I've been so fixated on what's happening now that my father's reaction and the potential consequences hadn't occurred to me.

'If Owen is involved in some way that's going to make things more difficult.'

I cringe at this. My father is suspicious enough of Owen as it is. If he has any reason to doubt him over what's occurred on the island, then he won't hesitate to do whatever it takes to ensure Owen is punished.

'We don't know for certain that it's Owen though...' My thoughts keep going back and forth on this. I should be more loyal to him. After all, don't they say innocent until proven guilty? And now I'm in safe surroundings and I've calmed down, I can put things in perspective a bit more. Owen is gentle, kind and sweet. Leo might have got it wrong.

Maybe he didn't see Owen kissing Astrid? Perhaps there's a reasonable explanation...

'He's obviously been lying to you,' Leo insists. 'Creeping around at night kissing other women for a start. But given he's romantically linked to Astrid, that's going to put him first in line for investigation.'

Leo's words feel like stabs to my heart.

'Don't open the door,' Leo says, dropping a kiss on my forehead. 'Stay here and I'll be back as soon as I can.'

***

The day has galloped on, somehow it's past lunchtime and I'm tucked into a bed in one of the unused rooms in the big guesthouse, the sheet up around my chin and my eyes squeezed shut even though I'm not remotely asleep. I can't stop thinking about Owen. The more I obsess about it, the more I wonder how the man who has been so loving towards me could cheat? He just doesn't seem the type. But then again, seeing him get so angry was a shock to the system. Maybe he's well and truly duped me? Perhaps my father's insinuation that he's after my fortune and doesn't really care about me is true.

I go over and over our relationship so far. I realise there's so much that I don't know about Owen. I've never met his friends and family, been to his hometown or even seen his social media profiles. He claims to be uninterested in having a social media presence, preferring to interact in real life instead. That's unusual for someone of his age. Is there a reason behind it? Or is the straight-forward, kind-hearted man I've spent the last few months with the true Owen?

I toss and turn in the bed. I'm trying to keep my paranoia at bay even though I just want to get off this island now. I never thought I'd feel like that about this place. But I feel trapped. My mind races through potential escape routes. Even though we have a helicopter landing pad, the helicopter isn't actually here as we arrived by boat this time. Both Leo's speedboat and my own boat are in the harbour, along with a few of the fishing boats used by the locals that we give permission to fish on the shores in exchange for buying their catches at reasonable rates. But none of those options are exactly quick getaways and, even though I could command a boat if needed, it's not up there with one of my highest skills.

I hear the front door open downstairs and I sit bolt upright. It must be Leo, but I still feel afraid. I'm tempted to jump in the wardrobe and hide myself away. If someone wanted to find me in here it wouldn't take much. So I sit on the edge of the bed, waiting.

'Leo? Leo?'

It's Hazel's voice. Leo said not to open the door to anyone but Hazel has a key and this house is her vacation accommodation, so I can't exactly tell her to go away.

Opening the door to the bedroom, I peer out. At the same time, Hazel reaches the top step. She eyes me suspiciously.

'You? What are you doing here?' I'm taken aback by brash tone of Hazel's voice. She pushes past me and flings open the bedroom door. 'Is Leo in here with you?'

'No, he isn't!'

Hazel flies through to the ensuite, checking in there too. Then she even opens the wardrobe I was about to hide in as well as making sure he's not under the bed. It dawns on me why she's doing this.

'Leo isn't here, Hazel. He's gone to find my bodyguards for me.'

Hazel folds her arms, looking frosty. 'Can't Owen do that for you?'

Before I have a chance to respond Hazel continues. 'You're spending an awful lot of time with *my* boyfriend for someone who's on their honeymoon.'

I lean on the doorframe and consider her thinly veiled accusation. I wasn't expecting her to query my relationship with Leo.

'Leo and I have known each other for a long time.'

'Yes, I'm aware.' Hazel's eyes are like slits and she flicks her silvery hair impatiently, as if she's waiting for a better answer.

'There's nothing going on between Leo and me.' I feel a red blush creeping up my neck as I say this. I don't know why I feel the need to justify myself. It's completely true, there's nothing going on. Leo confessed yesterday that he wished things hadn't fizzled out between us but that's as far as it went. I made it clear that it wasn't appropriate for him to share those feelings now that I'm married. Although, I do feel guilty that I've been dwelling on what might have been and that I ran to him earlier on today. But it's complicated. Leo wasn't just my lover, he was one of my closest confidents during my formative adult years. I don't have many friends, I don't have a huge circle of people around me. There are only a select few that I trust and Leo was one of them. Well, until he practically ghosted me when he was working out in Hong Kong.

I'm aware I'm standing slack-jawed. I can't dwell on these thoughts now.

'Hazel, something terrible has happened,' I blurt out, partly to change the subject and partly because I feel the need to warn her.

If I wasn't looking directly at her, I swear Hazel would be eye-rolling at me right now. I can tell she thinks this isn't going to be something worth worrying about.

'Someone has died.'

Hazel's eyes go wide in disbelief. 'Died?'

'One of the staff. She was found at the bottom of one of the cliffs on the north side of the island this morning.'

'That's awful,' Hazel says, sitting down on the edge of the bed. Her spikiness seems to subside a notch.

'Leo is worried someone on the island is responsible.'

'You mean, it wasn't suicide or an accident?' Hazel studies me intently.

'We don't know but we can't take any chances.'

Hazel holds my gaze, questioningly. A wave of sadness crashes over me once more and I stifle a sob as I think of the poor young woman who has lost her life.

'There's something else,' I add, my eyes brimming with tears. And then the information about Leo seeing Owen with Astrid the night before she died comes tumbling out. I'm not sure why I'm telling Hazel this, but I'm trying to untangle the information I have and I often find that speaking a problem out loud can help to solve it.

Hazel gapes at me. 'When did you find out that Owen had been with Astrid?'

'This morning, Leo told me.'

'Is that so?'

'Yes.' A tear leaks out and slides down my cheek. This still doesn't feel real. I thought Owen loved me. Maybe Leo got it all wrong? But I think back to the way Leo told me, he was adamant. And why would he lie?

Hazel stands up slowly and she's got that frosty look on her face again. 'So your husband cheated on you with one of the staff and now she's dead?'

'Um... no, it didn't happen like that,' I stutter. 'I only found out Owen and Astrid had kissed when Leo told me this morning.'

'Are you telling the truth?' Hazel narrows her green cat's eyes at me.

'Of course I am!'

I hear a noise outside and I cross my fingers that it's Leo with my bodyguards. Hazel looks worried, glancing between me and the open bedroom door.

'No offence, but I really don't know you at all,' Hazel moves further away from me, blocking the doorway.

'Exactly what do you mean by that?'

Hazel crosses her arms. 'How do I know that it wasn't you?'

My eyes go wide. 'How dare you!'

'Don't they say most murders are the result of money or love? If Owen was having an affair with Astrid, I'd say that gives you one big motive.'

The front door crashes open on the floor below. Hazel and I both jump.

My stomach flips over. She's right. I hadn't thought about it like that before. I only found out about Owen and Astrid kissing because Leo told me this morning. Leo will be able to tell anyone that.

But will anyone believe I hadn't found out before? Or will people wonder if I'm a jealous wife... and a killer?

Chapter Twenty-One
Owen

The rain has started to fall once more and the wind is getting stronger. I pull the golf buggy up in front of the guesthouse where I last saw Sienna. Leaping out of the buggy, I barrel my way through the unlocked front door. As I hurtle into the house, a woman bolts past me, without stopping.

I recognise straight away it's not Sienna: it's Hazel. Her distinctive silver hair billowing out behind her. I call her name several times but the words disappear in the wind and she doesn't stop. My heart thuds in my chest, what's going on now?

Joseph and Molly are right behind me. One of the pots containing a leafy plant has been knocked over, and soil and cracked pottery are scattered across the black and white tiles in the hallway.

'Oh dear, what a mess!' Molly tuts.

'Perhaps you better go first,' I say in a low voice to the older couple. I don't want a repeat of being kicked out again. I hope the Tanners will be able to pave the way for me to have a proper conversation with Sienna.

As we move along the hallway, I can hear the sound of crying coming from upstairs. My protective instincts kick in and, all thoughts of making things easier go out of my head, I just want to check my wife isn't hurt. I jerk forward, intending to start climbing the stairs but Molly puts her hand out.

'I'll deal with this,' she tells me.

The motherly woman heads up the stairs, Joseph just behind her. I admire how they're sticking together as a team and how they're not afraid to face whatever they need to in order to help their beloved Sienna.

They reach the top of the stairs quickly and I follow just behind them, in case I'm needed. I'm still fearful there's someone on this island who means Sienna harm. I just hope there isn't a murderer in this house...

Molly and Joseph disappear into the room where the crying is coming from. I pace along the hallway, sticking my head through each of the doorways leading into bedrooms and bathrooms. There's no sign of anyone else and Leo doesn't appear to be up here either, unless he's in the room the Tanners have just gone into.

Balling my fists tight, I wait, tense all over, willing Sienna to be okay. Eventually, Molly leads her out into the hallway. I can see immediately that my wife is still jittery. Her hair is dishevelled, her face is tear-stained but, thankfully, she appears unharmed. I let out a breath that I didn't know I was holding, releasing some of the tension from my body.

Joseph follows the two women out, but there's still no sign of Leo. Perhaps if he isn't here I might stand a chance to get Sienna to listen to me, instead of her being reeled in again by Leo's confident patter.

'Let's have a nice cup of tea and work out what to do next,' Molly says in her comforting voice, leading us all into the kitchen.

I scan the room, it's empty.

'Is Leo here?' I can't help myself; I have to know.

Sienna shakes her head, but doesn't look at me.

'He left you!' I explode with disgust. 'He said he was going to look after you!'

'He's gone to get my bodyguards,' Sienna mumbles. 'The phone lines are down.' She's fiddling with her silver bracelet and still avoiding eye contact with me.

'Ah, this storm has probably interrupted the connection,' Joseph comments.

The rain is now lashing down outside, pelting the windows while the wind rattles the shutters. It's mid-afternoon, but the skies are dark and a gloomy, dense fog hangs around the guesthouse. My eyes roam the room, there's something about this house that gives me the creeps. The furniture in here is dark and heavy, nothing like the modern feel of the interior of the villa. There are lots of little sculptures and ornaments dotted about the house and, while I can appreciate their artistic value, in the darker light of the afternoon I keep catching little eyes staring at me from clay models and stretched smiles gaping at me from wood carvings. I shiver.

Joseph turns on the light and Molly sets about making drinks. As I observe my surroundings, I notice there's a knife block on the kitchen worktop. There are six slots, but only five knives. I don't want to read too much in it but, just to be sure, I check the low butler sink. It's empty. The worktops are clear of clutter and the only other place I'm guessing the knife might be is in the dishwasher. I've just watched Molly taking milk from the fridge and gathering cups from a cupboard, and I take a guess at which of the kitchen cupboards possibly contains a dishwasher: the one with a handle at the top of the door rather than on the side. I'm right. But the dishwasher is completely empty.

I sit down heavily. I don't want to read too much into it but the knives on that block are sharp ones. Maybe one of the knives has been missing for a while, or blunt or broken. There could be lots of reasons why it's not there but I fear the worst-case scenario. The niggling voice inside my head is insisting the knife has fallen into the hands of someone who might use it as a weapon.

Molly doles out the tea. The scene in front of me could be a very normal one, the four of us gathering for a cosy chat. Except it's anything but. The future of my marriage could rest on the outcome of this conversation. I was planning to wait for Molly to take the lead, but I can't. I have to say something now Sienna is here in front of me.

'Sienna, it's me... I know you're frightened but I'm on your side.'

Sienna's shoulders seem to drop a little bit, her blue eyes meet mine but she says nothing.

'You married me, Sienna.' I hold out my left hand and I twist the gold band on my ring finger. 'I promised to love you and look after you, and I meant it.'

Sienna bites her lip. 'Swear to me you had nothing to do with Astrid's death.'

'I swear it.' I place my hand over my heart to show how sincere I am.

'At a time like this, it's natural to be wary,' Joseph says gently. 'But we're all here to keep you safe.' His gnarled fingers grasp Sienna's smooth, slim hand.

'Nothing is certain,' Molly's voice is measured. 'You know Joseph and I have your best interests at heart. You need to stick with us because

I don't want any harm to come to you,' she adds, her voice starting to shake.

Sienna bows her head tearfully.

'There's something you need to know,' Molly continues. 'Astrid was a troubled girl, she had lots of issues. I'm not saying she would've ended her own life like that but I am saying that we need to keep an open mind on the events that resulted in her death.'

'I'm sorry to hear that,' I say sincerely.

'Thank you,' Sienna looks up again, 'I know I can rely on the two of you.'

I feel as though my body has just received an electric shock. Sienna's meaning is clear: she trusts the Tanners but not me.

Molly leans over and gives Sienna a squeeze.

'Let's get you over to the villa,' Joseph says. 'I'll be a lot happier when we have your security team with us.'

As we all pass along the hallway, stepping over the shards of pottery and clumps of soil, I overhear Molly saying to Sienna: 'Owen here has a heart of gold. He'd do anything for you.'

I'm grateful Molly is trying to talk sense to Sienna.

Next I hear Molly asking, 'Do you really believe the man you married could have killed someone?'

As Molly is speaking, Joseph opens the front door and the fierce elements outside drown out Sienna's answer. I wish I knew what it was.

***

We hurry into the spacious porch area at the front of the villa, all four of us drenched to the bone. We were only outside for five minutes but the heavens opened and we may as well have stepped into a shower fully clothed. The flimsy roof of the golf buggy did nothing to protect us from the elements. Water pools on the white tiles beneath us. I peel off my t-shirt, which is heavy with water, exposing my bare chest.

Sienna is so close to me and I just want to reach out to her and fold her into my arms. But even though we're physically close, it feels like a wall has gone up between us. She's still not talking to me and I just have to hope it's not too late to fix things between us.

'Why don't you get changed,' Molly suggests to Sienna.

'What about you?' Sienna asks her.

'I've got a spare set of clothes in my cupboard. Owen, do you have anything Joseph could borrow?'

I'm frustrated we're having to take time to sort ourselves out but it's needed. I head up the staircase first, on high alert, not sure what I'm expecting to find. Everything is quiet.

I find Joseph some clothes and then I get changed quickly in the main bedroom. Sienna is dressing in another room. I'm almost done when I hear a sound that makes my blood run cold.

Someone is screaming.

Racing down the stairs, I follow the direction of the noise to the back of the villa and into the security room. My heart lurches as I take in the scene before me.

Sienna is on the floor, blood splatters beside her and dark red smears over both of her hands.

She is still screaming, her voice becoming higher in intensity. Behind her a body is lying prone on the ground.

'He's dead, he's dead!' Sienna cries.

I get a shudder of déjà vu. This is the second time today that I've found the woman I love next to a dead body.

I sidestep around her, being careful not to tread in any of the blood, trying to figure out exactly what's happened.

There on the floor is Bruce, Sienna's long-time bodyguard. His throat has been cut; a deep slit slashed into his neck. The blood is still oozing everywhere, which means he's only recently met his unfortunate end.

I feel nauseous and every fibre in my body is telling me to get away from here but I need to keep my cool and help Sienna. Surveying the room, I note there's no sign of a murder weapon anywhere. From the way poor Bruce has met his end, it seems a knife has been used. I shudder as I think of the empty slot in the knife block in the kitchen of the guesthouse we've just come from. Perhaps I'm overthinking the missing knife, maybe it's been absent for years, but I can't rule out anything at this point.

I also see the place has been ransacked. Drawers have been pulled open, there's paperwork everywhere, and the surveillance cameras have all been smashed. There's no sign of either Bruce or Kostas's laptops and I'm guessing whoever was in here was either trying to cover up their previous actions or ensuring their next move is not recorded.

It crosses my mind Sienna might be the killer. She's here, covered in Bruce's blood. And she also happened to be the first person to find Astrid's broken body as well. But I dismiss the thought as soon as it comes because I don't believe she is capable of ending someone's life. And there's no reason for her to kill Bruce, he was one of her most trusted employees.

Sienna is quietly crying now; she's trying to smooth Bruce's long hair back from his face but she's getting more blood everywhere. She looks stricken with grief as she fumbles for Bruce's wrist, presumably hoping to find a pulse, but it's very clear this man is dead.

'Sienna, you have to come away now.'

She whispers something to the prone body on the floor and it hits me just how much of a blow this must be to her. I know first-hand how present Bruce was in Sienna's life. It took a lot of devious planning from the pair of us to engineer some time to escape their watch and tie the knot in our hasty beach ceremony in Cuba. Bruce has been her protector, her friend, her confidante. Now he's gone.

Losing anyone close to you is devastating, but losing someone you spend day in and day out with in such a sudden and brutal way like this is terrible. But I can't dwell on emotions. It's obvious there's a killer in our midst now.

I need to act and find whoever did this – and prevent the murderer from striking again.

Before anyone else dies.

Chapter Twenty-Two
Sienna

I'm covered in blood. Dark, sticky, warm blood that seeps into my clothes and congeals under my fingernails. Bruce's slack face swims before me and I try to blink away the hot tears that are starting to fall. I don't think I'll ever be able to erase this horrific experience from my memories. It was one thing seeing Astrid, an employee I only knew briefly, dead at the bottom of those steep steps. But being up close to Bruce's mutilated form, his blood still flowing, flicks a switch of pure terror in my brain.

I can hear screaming. I'm aware the sound is coming from me but I can't seem to stop myself.

That is, until Owen steps in the room. When he found me near Astrid's body I was afraid, out there on the slippery steps with a sheer drop on one side and no-one else nearby. Now, I feel the total opposite. I'm glad he's come to my aid once more. I need his help more than ever.

Suddenly there's a rush of activity. I'm aware of someone standing in the doorway.

'Jed,' Owen speaks in a clear and authoritative voice. 'Go and get Molly and Joseph.'

Eventually, Owen coaxes me away from Bruce. I can't believe I won't see his face again. Although Bruce appeared surly and serious, he had a dry sense of humour and he was the most loyal man I know. He never married, but he had a mother and a sister who he made sure were financially comfortable. He used to tell me about his visits to his mother's home in Yorkshire. It sounded like he was from a close-knit family, there were always lots of people piled into his mother's cottage at Christmastime. He showed me photos of his niece and nephews. Who will break the news to them? How will they cope knowing Bruce was murdered?

These are the thoughts occupying me as Owen guides me to a small bathroom adjacent to the security room. He twists the tap and places my hands under the running water. We both watch the blood running down the plughole. Owen squeezes soap over my hands. Gently and carefully he sets about scrubbing off the blood until finally the water runs clear. I then shed the light t-shirt I was wearing, which is now covered in splattered blood. My sports vest below is untarnished.

'Thank you,' I stutter, meaning it. I wish we could wind the clock back twenty-four hours. My feelings for Owen run deep but I have to be cautious. The way he's behaving doesn't suggest he has any murderous intentions towards me, but I don't know that for sure.

Molly and Joseph arrive, they both look ruffled and unlike their usually organised selves. Owen goes to speak with them. I don't hear what he says, but they both scurry off. Clearly they have jobs to do now we're going to need to alert the mainland to not one but two dead bodies. However, with the storm raging and the phone lines down our only other method of communication is via the high-tech security room. Except that's all smashed up now.

Owen leads me out of the security room and away from Bruce. I can't look in his direction again. I can't bear to see the life extinguished from someone I knew so well and spent so much time with. I'm devastated.

Owen's behaving so tenderly, he's looking after me in such a considerate way and his actions are making me question all the doubts I've been having about him. I don't feel scared or afraid to be near the man I married. Earlier on, the shock of seeing Astrid's body sent me into flight mode. Finding Bruce has left me on the brink of a meltdown and I crave to step into Owen's arms. I badly want him to hold me and tell me this madness is going to stop. My head is all over the place and my heart is telling me to trust my husband.

But how can I trust anyone right now? Owen had a piece of the fuchsia dress in his hand and flared up in anger outside the guesthouse. Leo, I've known forever but he's been very quick to try and put the blame on someone else. I trust Molly and Joseph with my life but there are other members of staff, like Jed, who I'm now more wary of. Then there's Kostas, where is he in all of this? All these contradictions and possibilities are hammering against each other in my skull but the truth of what's been happening evades me.

I nervously follow Owen outside, running my fingers over the familiar shapes attached to my charm bracelet as I go. We head past the games room and go out under the covered bar area where we sit on stools. The rain is lashing around us but there's enough protection from the elements here, for now. Owen's face is so close to mine and I think he's going to dip his head down and kiss me but he doesn't.

'Here,' Owen says, handing me a tumbler with a shot of whisky in it.

Swigging back the amber liquid, I relish the familiar taste hitting the back of my throat. My hand shakes as I place the glass down.

Now Owen is here, his solid frame and his gorgeous face in front of me, my brain seems to have unfogged, despite the shocking discovery of Bruce, and I'm thinking clearly for the first time today. Leo's words about Owen kissing Astrid are imprinted on my mind but I need to give Owen the benefit of the doubt and a chance to explain himself.

'Molly and Joseph are sorting out Bruce,' Owen tells me. 'Jed and Diego, the IT guy, are trying to get one of the devices in the security room up and running again so we can send word that we need help. I'm going to do everything I can to keep you safe.'

'Why?'

'Because I love you.'

'The way I behaved earlier though...'

'You were scared. And, given everything that's happened to you in the past, I don't blame you.'

Owen is saying all the right things, but does he mean them?

'I'm sorry,' I say slowly. 'It was wrong of me to behave in the way I did earlier.' I don't know what I'm apologising for more, accusing him of pushing Astrid or running to Leo. 'It's just... when I saw you holding that piece of Astrid's dress, I put two and two together and...'

'I get it. Look, can I just tell you how things seem from where I'm standing?'

I bite my lip. Perhaps now Owen is going to tell me the truth about him and Astrid. I begin to shake, I'm not sure that I'm ready to hear this.

'You're cold.' Owen takes off the light sweater he's wearing and gives it to me. I accept, inhaling the scent of him as the material fits to my body. I really don't want Owen to say something that's going to end our marriage. Being with him is reinforcing how hard I fell for him and how much I wanted our relationship to work. But I have to hear this.

'We don't know what happened to Astrid yet but, given the situation with Bruce, we have to face the fact there's someone on the island who could be a threat to all of us, especially you.' He takes a deep breath. 'A woman with similar physical features to you has been killed as well as one of your bodyguards.'

'And we haven't seen Kostas yet.' This has been bothering me since I saw the security room all smashed up. Kostas may have been hurt or worse too. I'm feeling jittery about his whereabouts because, if he is still alive, he could be the killer's next target. It would make sense they'd want to take out the people protecting me, if getting to me is their end goal.

A cloud passes over Owen's face. 'I hadn't thought of that,' he admits.

'There are any number of people on this island who could be responsible. I've been wracking my brains and I've got a list of those I want to work out the whereabouts of.' Owen's talking hurriedly now, his foot jangling up and down in agitation. He keeps checking all around him and his sudden nervous energy is starting to make me feel even more frightened.

'The Italian couple Molly mentioned were staying here, where are they? Don't you think it's weird they didn't even say hello to us? Are they still on the island?'

I screw up my face trying to remember. 'I think they were meant to be leaving today. I can check with Molly.'

'Well, with the weather like this I'm not sure if they will have been able to leave. They might still be here. We don't know anything about them so we have to find out if they're on the island or not.'

'They've only been here for a short while. Why would they want to... to kill Astrid and Bruce?'

'We don't know who they are. They could be people who have a grudge against your father.'

A shiver runs down my spine. I've been in circumstances like these before, where complete strangers wish me harm because of something my father has said or done. Owen is right, we have to keep every possibility in mind.

'We need to work out if any of the staff might be responsible. I spoke to Molly and Joseph earlier and there wasn't anyone they could think of. But two members of staff have died now, so it's possible that an employee here is seeking some kind of revenge.'

I study Owen, his strong features, his thick, dark hair and chocolate-brown eyes. I want to put my trust in him. But he's just given two examples that could point the finger at him. He is more of an unknown quantity to me than many people on this island, who I've known for years. And he was also one of the staff. My stomach is doing somersaults again.

'Then there's Leo. We don't know where he is now and he was meant to be going to security for help.'

'Owen, maybe Leo has been hurt as well? If he was here when Bruce was murdered?' Even though Leo and I aren't a couple any more, even though he broke my heart, I wouldn't wish him ill. Even though he thinks of himself first, I don't believe he is a killer. And if anything has happened to him because of me...

'I thought that might be your response,' Owen says, folding his arms across his chest.

'Leo could be in danger!' I know I'm coming across as far too defensive now.

'Leo isn't just your father's employee, is he?' Owen asks, swallowing.

'I've known Leo for a long time.' This conversation is veering off in a direction I'm not comfortable with.

'Have you and Leo ever been an item?' Owen is standing now, towering above me, and his question is so direct, so hard-hitting, that at first it throws me completely.

'I'll take that as a yes then,' Owen curls his lip.

'It's not that simple,' I say. 'But we were never officially an item.'

'But you did sleep together?'

'Owen!' I'm on my feet now, anger flaming inside me.

'Why didn't you just tell me that?' Owen asks me in his deep, gravelly voice.

'It's not exactly the sort of thing you drop into a casual chat on your honeymoon, is it? "Oh that guy you just spoke to, I slept with him."'

'I'm your husband, I thought you would be honest with me.'

'It's in the past,' I snap, annoyed he is making a big deal of this. 'Leo made it clear he didn't want a relationship. And I married you because I realised I didn't want to be with someone like Leo Harrison. You were so different to anyone I've met before. And I fell for you straight away...'

My eyes are glittering with tears again and I'm so mad because Owen is standing here grilling me about Leo, about things that happened a long time ago, and yet he still hasn't told me the truth about Astrid.

'Why did you have to go and ruin it, Owen?'

'Me!' Owen is pacing up and down now. 'Ever since Leo arrived, you've done nothing but flirt with him.'

'I haven't *kissed* him.'

Owen comes to a halt. 'What do you mean by that?'

'When were you going to tell me, Owen?' I jab him in the chest as I speak. 'When were you going to admit to kissing Astrid?' I'm fuming now. I felt bad for jumping to conclusions about my husband earlier but why is he interrogating me about Leo at a time like this? Particularly when he's been seen with another woman.

Owen's face falls. Instinctively, I can tell this is the truth.

'Oh my God! So you did kiss her then!' I'd been clinging onto the idea that Leo had somehow misinterpreted what he saw.

'Who told you that?' he barks at me.

I step back, feeling afraid. If this is true, if Owen really did kiss Astrid and cheated on me then he isn't the man I thought he was. If my judgement about Owen has been completely off then perhaps I really don't know him at all. And perhaps he did kill Astrid. My brain is in overdrive once more.

'It doesn't matter who told me.' My voice is barely a whisper. 'What matters is whether you did it or not.'

A small part of me is still holding out, still hoping that he will deny it and that it won't be true.

'This is so messed up!' Owen avoids the question, ducks behind the bar and pours himself some rum. He downs it in one swift movement.

He paces up and down the deck for a few moments before he finally turns to face me. I should just go now and get as far away from Owen Turner as I can. Except, there's something still pulling me towards him. The invisible thread of our marriage runs between us, and I'm waiting with bated breath, wanting him to say something that will magically make all of this better.

'I should have told you this before,' he says. 'You have to believe me; it's not how it seems.'

'Oh! You seriously aren't going to use that line, are you?' I gape at him, a pure rage building inside me. I thought Owen and I were going to be forever. Instead, he's beginning to convince me that everyone else around me was right about him.

'Sienna, listen. Astrid kissed me.'

I wasn't expecting him to say this and the admission stops me in my tracks.

'I went out for a walk. I saw a woman ahead of me, I thought it was you. Her hair colour... it was exactly the same shade. We'd just argued and I wanted to hold you, for us to make up. So I went up to her – thinking she was you – and cuddled her from behind. Just like we always do. Except that's when I realised it was the wrong woman.'

'And you expect me to believe that?' I sigh.

'Yes. It's the truth. I apologised to her but she read the signals all wrong and she kissed me. I told her it was a mistake and we parted ways. That was it.'

'So why didn't you tell me?' I should just drop this, but I can't seem to let it go. I want to understand fully so I can make my own mind up about where this leaves our marriage.

'I didn't think it mattered… it was a genuine mix-up. On my part anyway. I just wanted to forget about it.'

'And why didn't you tell me about it after she died?' I persist.

'Sienna, you already thought I had something to do with the body. I didn't want to make things worse.'

I gulp, he's digging himself a deeper and deeper hole. 'Owen, how do you expect me to trust you now?'

He closes the gap between us and takes one of my hands in his.

'You didn't exactly give me a chance to say anything just after you found Astrid. You ran from me… this is the first opportunity I've had to talk properly.'

He's right, I didn't give him that chance. So I allow him to keep holding onto my hand and I listen to what he has to say next.

'I'm well aware that Astrid coming onto me, followed by me turning her away, is going to be viewed suspiciously. I had nothing to do with her death though and I certainly didn't have anything to do with Bruce's. I promise you.'

My emotions are running riot. I'm swinging from feeling sorry for Owen and being furious with him. I don't know what to think. Memories of us sneaking down to that very lagoon, frolicking in the clear water together and then having a picnic on the white sand beach, assault my senses. Now we're together again, I feel less fearful. I don't feel afraid of him. But that doesn't mean I can trust him.

'I want to protect you. I want to make sure that you stay safe,' Owen says, his voice full of tenderness.

I look into his brown eyes and my heart wants to believe him, but my mind is still telling me to be more cautious.

'I can't stand the thought that you don't trust me. What happened to us?'

Owen is welling up now. What if everything he is saying is true and I'm being the worst wife ever?

But what if he's lying? And what if I'm playing into his plan? I could still be in danger right now.

I move away abruptly, snatching my hand out of his, my sparkling engagement ring catching on the soft skin of his palm in my haste to put some space between us.

'I've got to go.' I whisper and start walking away, knowing I can't look back in case it shakes my resolve.

'Sienna, don't leave!'

Chapter Twenty-Three
Owen

'Having a bad day?'

Jed appears only seconds after Sienna disappears from my line of sight and into the villa. It's clear he's listened to some of the conversation between us. But exactly how much did he hear?

'Jed, just leave it.'

'In trouble already, are we? I had a bet on that your marriage would last a year, don't make me lose it.' He sneers at me.

Grabbing Jed by the shirt, I shove him up against the wall. He's right, I am having a bad day and I don't need him to make it any worse.

'I said: leave it.'

'Let me go,' Jed says steadily, with more courage than I would've expected from him.

I come to my senses and relax my grip and let Jed wiggle away. To his credit, he didn't appear at all ruffled by my actions.

'You shouldn't have done that,' Jed tells me, his trademark smirk riling me up once more. He then waves his phone in my direction. 'That's all been voice recorded.'

'What! You little—'

I lunge for him. Jed has been winding me up since I arrived back on the island and he's taken it too far now.

Jed swerves and takes off, towards the outdoor pool.

I don't have the energy to run after him. I feel drained from the events of today and, even if I did catch up with him and teach him a lesson, I'd probably just end up landing myself in more trouble. And he's the last of my problems.

I want to keep talking to Sienna, to make her see that I'm innocent. But she's so emotional and nothing I'm saying is getting through to her. So, I've got to try a different tactic. The only way to save my name and to keep Sienna safe is to find out who the killer really is.

I'm not prepared to give up without a fight. I don't want Sienna to think I'm some kind of cold-blooded murderer or a cheat. I want her to know how much I love her, and that I'd do anything for her.

As I dust myself down, dark thoughts swirl around my brain. I'm worried this is going to be the end of my marriage and possibly my freedom too. After all, I'm the imposter, the person who doesn't fit in around here. I'm different and therefore that singles me out from the crowd.

It's times like these I wish I still smoked. I pull a chewing gum out from my pocket and get to work on that instead. The other thing I can't stop thinking about is the secret in my past I've hidden from Sienna, from the Tanners and the rest of the staff. If a police investigation gets underway, and I'm under fire, it's bound to come out and that will make things even worse.

The odds feel very highly stacked against me right now. So I've got to find out who's really responsible for the two deaths in order to save my own skin. The first person I'm going to start with is Leo. He promised to look after Sienna and then he vanished. The security room, where he was headed for, is trashed and one of the bodyguards dead. So he is top of my list.

I have one more shot of rum and then begin to scour the downstairs of the villa. I'm assuming that Sienna won't leave here now, and I'm hoping she's gone straight to our bedroom. In which case, I want to know exactly who else is in this building.

And I don't have to look too far.

I find Leo in the dining room, looking sweaty and pale, like he's had a shock.

'I told you to look after Sienna and you left her on her own.' I'm not beating around the bush any more. There's no time to waste with a killer on the loose and my marriage on the line.

Leo glares at me. 'Not you again.'

'I don't know what your problem is, but I want to know why you left my wife by herself and why one of the security guards is now dead?'

I square up to him. Leo is slightly shorter than me and a lot slimmer. He spends most of his time tap-tapping at a keyboard and going to swanky lunches, so I'm not expecting him to be any kind of match for me, someone who has spent the majority of their adult working life doing manual labour and much of their spare time in the gym.

Leo takes a step closer to me. 'Maybe you should be asking yourself why your wife came to me in the first place?'

My fist connects with Leo's face. There's no thought behind it. I'm already angry from my exchange with Jed and Leo is now receiving the full force of my wrath.

Leo staggers back and lands on the tiled floor, his head narrowly missing the edge of the worktop on his way down.

'What the hell?'

Blood is pouring out of Leo's nose. I don't feel guilty at all, I've been wanting to do that since the first night I met him.

'You'll be hearing from my lawyer!' Leo bleats. 'If you've broken my nose, then you'll pay.'

I step towards him, crouching down so our eyes are level. 'That's just a taste of what I can do, Leo. You have no idea who I really am. If you ever come near my wife again—'

'Leo!'

Sienna flies across the room, a look of horror on her face. 'Leo, are you okay?'

She shoulders me out the way and starts fussing around my rival.

'What were you thinking?' She turns to glare at me and then her eyes widen. 'You weren't about to…?' She looks genuinely terrified of me and it breaks my heart.

'He came out of nowhere, hit me for no reason.' Leo allows Sienna to help him to his feet and I spring back, away from them.

Leo's nose is bleeding quite a lot and Sienna hands him a cloth to staunch the flow. Leo's face may be bloodied but he's the one who's come out the victor in this scenario.

There's nothing I can say. My wife leads Leo out of the room, not looking back at me.

I'd bet my life that Leo was deliberately goading me. He probably knew Sienna was close by. He's the second person who's set me up this afternoon.

And perhaps he's not just set me up for this.

Perhaps Leo's been planning for me to take the fall for the murders all along.

Chapter Twenty-Four
The Killer

Only one person was supposed to die today. And she's still alive.

I haven't done this out of choice. I didn't intend to slit Bruce's throat but I have a right to defend myself. That man was dangerous. He was on to me, so it was my life or his.

If it means that Sienna is less well protected now? Well that's just an added bonus.

With this storm driving everyone indoors, she'll never suspect anything until it's too late. I wonder if she's scared? I hope so. She deserves to suffer after everything she's done, after all the grief she's caused me.

I want to be clear about this: I'm out for revenge. But I'm doing the right thing here. I want to right a wrong.

To do that Sienna has to die, along with anyone trying to protect her from me.

I'm going to make sure she never leaves this island.

And I'll kill anyone else who stands in my way.

Chapter Twenty-Five
Sienna

'Are you okay?' I check Leo over; it's just his nose that's bleeding but it's pretty bad. 'Come and sit down. Lean forward, it will help.'

We're in the sunroom at the front of the house. I've always loved this space, with its floor-to-ceiling windows and enormous skylight. It's usually filled with sunshine all day long but it's also fitted with an air-con unit and two ceiling fans so it also remains nice and cool. It's the perfect part of the house to come to if you want respite from the heat outside. Except now, with the wind howling all around the villa and the rain battering the windows, the whole room is transformed and feels much more exposed to the elements.

Lightning cracks above us followed by a deep roll of thunder. I jump in response to the booming sound overhead. I'm completely traumatised after being covered in Bruce's blood earlier. The sunroom is only just along the hallway from the security room and close to the front entrance of the building. I'm on edge being in this part of the villa, especially after seeing the results of Owen's handiwork and knowing he isn't far away. I want to move us to a different space, but Leo is still hunched over.

I watch as one, two, three droplets of blood hit the pristine white tiles. The red looks so stark against the clean tile, and it makes me even more anxious to get out of here.

'How are you doing?' I ask softly.

Leo sits up. His eyes are still bloodshot and the bottom half of his face is caked in blood but the flow seems to have eased up a bit now.

'I've been better,' he jokes feebly. 'Does my nose look broken?'

Inspecting his face, I try to see through the blood and swelling, but it's hard to tell. 'I think we need to get you cleaned up to have a proper look.'

Leo winces. 'Not my nose.'

I can't help but smile at this. Leo is so vain, so the idea of having a crooked nose will not sit well with him. I can see him rushing straight to a plastic surgeon, even if it's only slightly out of joint.

Another bright crack of lightning shoots through the dark sky above us.

'I don't want to stay in this room,' I whisper.

'Okay, do you want to go back to mine... I mean the guesthouse?'

We both look out at the torrential rain, it's getting worse. 'No, I need to go up to my room, there's something I have to get.'

Leo stands up, he wobbles slightly.

'I'm so sorry. What Owen did...'

'It's not your fault,' Leo says, taking my arm when I offer it to him. 'But I hope you can now see the kind of man you married.'

I bite my tongue and stop myself from saying anything. Leo is in pain and he has every right to be angry with Owen but there's something about the way he says this that comes across as too smug, even for Leo. Even though I'm feeling so mixed up about my husband, especially after seeing what he just did to Leo, I want to make my own decisions about him.

We take the stairs slowly, Leo still pinching the top of his nose with his fingers. With each step we take, I get visions of every horror movie I've ever watched. When the victim goes up the stairs, I'm screaming for them to get out of the house. Internally, I'm screaming at myself to do the same right now. But I have to get up to my room, there's something I need from my safe, and once I have it I can protect myself much better.

When we get into the bedroom, I slide the lock across and also grab a chair and shove it up against the door. Leo slumps down on the edge of the bed and I wince as I see more red droplets spraying over the white bedspread.

All day I've been feeling emotional, with tears falling at each new horrifying turn of events. Now I realise I need to take charge. I can't wait on Kostas being found alive, I can't rely on getting word to the mainland, and I can't trust any of the staff when there could be a killer amongst them. I'm horrified by Owen's behaviour just now and Leo has just demonstrated that it doesn't take much to knock him down. So it's up to me to protect myself. Every fibre of my being is on high alert and I know what I need to do to try to survive the night. This situation is the stuff of nightmares, and only I can get myself out of paradise alive.

The storm is still raging outside and it's clearly not stopping any time soon. Given the bend of the palm trees that I can see from the window and the sound of the turbulent sea in the backdrop, there's no way I can risk escaping outside now. And nightfall has just arrived, increasing the darkness all around the villa. So there's only one place I can go where I'll feel safe. And that's to the villa's inbuilt panic room that's hidden in a vaulted space in the basement.

All I need is the key.

Leo is hunched over again, hanging his head forward and moaning. So first I run a flannel under the cold tap in the bathroom and hand it to him.

'This might help to take the sting away.'

With Leo preoccupied, I move to the far end of the room. My safe is hidden behind a panel in the wall. Looking at the wall you'd never guess it's there as it's been so cleverly concealed. I press the square area with my fingerprint and the panel unfolds slowly. I glance over my shoulder to check that Leo isn't looking this way, but he's far too busy mopping up his face.

So I quickly enter the combination number and pop open the metal door of the safe. The key isn't something I've ever needed before but I know it's in here, right at the back in a small, rectangular case.

Pushing a wad of money and some jewellery boxes out of the way, I reach as far as I can and swipe my hand around, expecting my fingers to touch upon the long box.

But it's not there.

Checking over my shoulder again, I watch as Leo goes into the bathroom. I click on the little light inside the safe and scan the interior. I note the money and the five jewellery boxes once more along with a bigger container, which holds a small gun. But there's no rectangular box for the key.

Moving the contents of the safe around, I try to remain calm, telling myself that the key must be in there somewhere. I feel all around the safe, just in case the key has somehow come out of the box, but it's definitely not there.

Alarm swirls inside me. I think back, trying to picture when I last opened the safe and what was in it. I barely ever switch the little light on though because usually I'm just dipping my hand in to get one of the jewellery boxes. I can't remember seeing the key box during the last week.

'Nice. A secret safe.'

Leo is behind me; I clang the door shut.

'Don't worry, I won't tell anyone,' he says, reading my mind, and then he takes in the expression on my face.

'What's wrong?'

'The key... there's a key I need and it's not there.'

'Are you sure?'

'Yes, I've checked thoroughly and it's gone.'

'Who else has access to the safe?'

'Only me and my father.'

'Not Owen?'

'He doesn't even know it's here.' My father has always instilled in me the need to keep this safe a secret. Apart from the significant amount of cash that's kept in here for emergencies, he has told me time and time again the gun should stay hidden for my protection and the panic room should not become common knowledge on the island.

'Someone must have taken it if it's not there.' Leo stating the obvious isn't helpful. 'Is there anyone else who knows about it?' he asks.

'There are only two other people my father may have told. Molly and Joseph.'

'Why would they have taken the key?'

'It's the key to the panic room.'

Leo's jaw drops slightly. 'Ah, I see.'

'Perhaps they've gone to open it up...' My voice trails away, I hope this explanation is correct.

'Let's stay here for a bit longer then. See if they come up to us.'

It's the only option available to me. If I haven't got the key to the panic room, then barricading myself in my room is the only thing I can do.

'I'm going back into the bathroom to finish cleaning up.' As Leo heads off in the direction of the bathroom, I wonder if he's being a tiny bit nonchalant. Then again, he's probably still obsessing over his nose.

When the bathroom door clicks shut, I turn back to the safe. I take out the gun and a fistful of notes, in case I need either in the coming hours.

While Leo is still in the other room, I hastily get changed into a pair of trousers, a fresh top and a light hoodie. If I do need to flee, this will be better attire to get caught outside in. Next, I take out my waist bag out of the bedside cabinet door and tie it around me, underneath my hoodie, tucking the money and gun inside.

When Leo emerges out of the bathroom, I'm sitting at my dressing table, trying to get my mobile phone to connect. But it's no use. The lines of communication are well and truly down thanks to this storm.

'No joy with the phone?' Leo asks me. His face is completely clean, which emphasises the swelling around his nose, and I can see the beginnings of a black eye beginning to form on his right side.

I sigh in response.

'I can't get any signal either,' he claims. 'I guess we're just going to have to wait things out now. There's nothing we can do until the morning.'

Leo is usually so in control. He's the sort of person who not only has a plan A, but will have a plan B and C up his sleeve just in case as well. So it strikes me as odd that he isn't taking the initiative and coming up with something more proactive than just waiting things out.

This room, with its enormous king size bed, walk-in wardrobe and luxurious ensuite, has always been a safe haven for me. I hope it continues to be so and we can stay protected here but there's absolutely no way I'm going to be able to go to sleep tonight, however tired I might be.

Leo closes the shutters, blocking out the extreme weather outside, and sits down on the two-seater sofa, positioned under the window. 'Come here,' he says, patting the cushion next to him.

Exhausted, I do as he says, plopping down on the seat. Leo immediately gathers me to him, putting his arm around me. I should resist but I don't. I lay my head on his shoulder and close my eyes. I'm reminded of all the times we spent in our early twenties, curled up on the sofa together. We were seeing each other but not officially dating. When I think back, we were always at my house or Leo's flat. We never went out anywhere together, in case we were seen, so the entirety of our relationship was conducted in secrecy and within the same two locations. I used to think it was romantic, but looking back I can see it was unhealthy behaviour.

'We're going to get everything sorted out,' Leo tells me in a soothing voice. 'But you may have to face the fact that Owen is involved in all of this.'

My heart quickens at my husband's name. Leo is tapping straight into my own fears, but I don't appreciate him stirring things up. I want to make my own mind up about Owen. This afternoon he didn't exactly convince me that he's innocent but, then again, the way he spoke and looked at me when we were outside all felt so genuine. In another few minutes, I may have decided to stay by his side. I'm so conflicted about whether to trust him. Everything has been turned upside down.

'He cheated on you and then tried to cover it up. He's just shown us he's got a nasty temper; I don't want you going anywhere near him again.'

The Owen I fell in love with is nothing like the person Leo is trying to paint. I keep thinking something isn't adding up here, but I can't put my finger on exactly what it is.

'He's dangerous,' Leo goes on. He's paid to be persuasive for a living, and it's clear he's going to keep hammering this view of Owen until I agree with him.

Leo is sounding more and more like my father, which makes me bristle. I wonder if he's trying a little too hard to lay the blame at Owen's door? Leo told me on the first night he was here that he regretted what we had between us was over. But would he go as far as to pile the blame on someone who's innocent just to get his way?

And then he says something that makes my heart skip a beat.

'Anyone investigating this is going to hear that Owen argued with Astrid the night before and that you saw him with a piece of her dress in his hand when you found the body and it will be case closed.'

My heart rate speeds up again. I'm absolutely certain that I didn't tell Leo about the fuchsia material of Astrid's dress. So how does he know this?

Pulling away from him, for the first time I wonder if Leo has something to do with the murders.

Has he been lying to me all along?

Chapter Twenty-Six
Owen

'Kostas!'

The bodyguard staggers into the villa, and I move forward to support him. He's panting heavily.

'Are you hurt?'

He inhales sharply, holding onto his side. Molly and Joseph rush towards us from the other end of the hallway, both of them moving as fast as they can.

'I'm fine,' Kostas croaks, as we stagger towards the kitchen, the bodyguard leaning his weight on me. 'Just a stitch. The storm has been raging out there, although it's just starting to die down. I shouldn't have gone out, but I had to.'

Molly and Joseph give each other a worried glance. They're probably thinking the same thing I am: does he know Bruce is dead?

'I was upstairs and I heard Bruce shout,' Kostas says, taking the towel that Molly offers him and beginning to dry his face and hair. 'And then there was a stretched, gurgling sound. I'd never heard anything like it in all the time we've worked together, so I knew it wasn't good.'

'I'm sorry,' Molly says, laying a hand on his shoulder.

'He was one of the best,' Kostas sniffs.

'Have this,' Joseph says, passing him a can of beer. Kostas cracks it open and takes a long gulp.

'Did you see who did it?' I ask him. The information could be vital in keeping everyone else safe.

'Yes and no,' Kostas answers. 'I came into the security office to find it being ransacked. Whoever it was had a balaclava on and was wearing dark clothes. I wasn't able to see their face.'

He takes another swig of his beer. 'When I got into the office, Bruce was already dead...'

'You did what you could,' Molly's voice is kind and heartfelt.

'I chased them out of the villa and I very nearly caught up with them, but I slipped in the rain and they got away.' Kostas drains the rest of the can and then crunches it up in his fist. 'I'll do whatever it takes to catch them.'

'What about height? Build?'

'A bit shorter than me, so tallish. And an average build. Not much to go on, I'm afraid.'

'Let's make sure the villa is secure for now. Where's Sienna?'

'She's up in her room, I saw her go up there earlier.' Molly hesitates, as if she wants to say something more.

'What is it?'

'She's with Leo,' Molly admits.

'At least we know where she is and we can keep an eye,' Joseph says.

'I don't trust him though,' I growl.

'I'm with you there,' Molly supports me. 'I'll head up there now and try to talk some sense into her.'

'Thank you, Molly.' I'm grateful to have her on my side.

'Let's do a once-over of the villa, secure everything.' I suggest. If the storm is dying down then maybe we might be able to get some signal or connection soon.'

Kostas stands up. 'I'll check outside, seeing as I'm already soaked through.'

'I'll come with you,' I say to him.

We leave Joseph and Molly in the villa and head outside and check all along the boundary first. The gated wall is secure and there's been no damage from the wind. We then start to check all the downstairs windows and doors are locked up.

'So Leo's trying to win Sienna back then?' Kostas says.

I grimace. This is confirmation, as if I needed any, that something had gone on between Sienna and Leo previously. Kostas, being one of Sienna's regular bodyguards, would no doubt have seen the whole thing played out.

'He's a slimy piece of work that guy is,' Kostas continues. 'He kept stringing Sienna along while it suited him but as soon as that job opportunity in Hong Kong came up, he was off.'

That sounds like it fits, given what I've seen of Leo so far. 'And I guess he thought he'd come back and pick up where he left off?'

'I'd say that was about right. Bet it was a bit of a shock to his ego to find out she'd married the gardener in his absence,' Kostas laughs, but not unkindly. 'No harm meant.'

I wave away his apology to let him know it's fine.

'Although, even if you hadn't come on the scene, I don't think she would've got back with him.'

'Really?' Hope blooms in my chest.

'No, he broke her heart and I don't think Sienna would give him another chance.'

'Not unless she thought her husband was a murderer and was now cosied up in a bedroom with her ex,' I reply gloomily.

Kostas looks at me with shock on his face. 'Sienna thinks you could be responsible?'

I nod my head in confirmation.

We check our last window and head back inside again. Even though the rain has eased off, it's still too wet to be outside for long.

Making our way through each of the downstairs rooms, my mood sinks lower and lower. Only a few days ago, I was getting used to this incredible villa in the sun. I couldn't believe this was my new way of life. I thought it was too good to be true, and I was right. I've never had much luck in my life, getting a job on Oyster Island and meeting Sienna were the first really positive things to happen to me. It looks like I'm going to lose it all now. If Sienna has sided with Leo for the second time today, then it doesn't look good for me, despite Kostas's opinion.

'Tell me about what's gone on,' Kostas says. 'It looks like we're in for a long night so we've got plenty of time.'

Kostas is employed as Sienna's protector, so it occurs to me that he may just be pumping me for information to see if there's any truth in Sienna's concerns. But I could do with talking to someone about this mess and he's my only option. Plus, my aim is to try and work out who the killer is and Kostas, given his profession, is probably my best shot at helping do this.

Explaining the events of the last couple of days to Kostas is uncomfortable. I don't want to admit arguments and mistakes, but if there's just a glimmer of possibility this might get him on my side and help me to unmask the murderer then it's worth it.

I go through the order of events with him. Kostas listens, without interrupting. He's the younger of the two bodyguards. Bruce was older, nearing retirement age, whereas Kostas looks like he's in his early forties, probably only about ten years older than me. As I speak, it's a relief to get everything off my chest and Kostas doesn't seem to be judging me in any way.

'Sheesh!' Kostas pats me on the arm. 'That's quite the situation you have there.' He looks thoughtful. 'From what you've said, it couldn't have been you who attacked Bruce. You were with Molly, Joseph and Sienna around the time it happened. And...' he looks me up and down, 'the person who killed Bruce wasn't as muscular as you. They were average build. Assuming we're just looking for one murderer, and not multiple, if you didn't kill Bruce then it's unlikely you killed Astrid.'

I exhale with relief. At least someone seems to believe my story.

'Although the events with Astrid are going to be harder to explain away...'

'I get it. None of it looks good.'

'That's true but it doesn't mean you're guilty.'

'Cheers Kostas. I just need to find out who *is* guilty, that's the only way to stop this madness.'

'I agree.' He scratches his head. 'You know what you could do...'

'Any ideas would be appreciated at this point, mate.'

'If you think Leo is behind the murders, why don't you go and do a bit of digging while he's occupied?'

'He's occupied with my wife!' I splutter.

'Molly will talk some sense into her and I'll be here with them. It might be your only chance to have a snoop around before something else happens... or the police descend on the island.'

I roll my tongue round in my mouth, weighing up the idea. I definitely think Leo is dodgy, and he certainly wants me out of the picture. But is he the killer?

He may have pushed Astrid off the cliff, perhaps to frame me? Or maybe he had another reason to target her. Why Bruce though? Perhaps whoever it was had tried to destroy some of the surveillance videos, to get rid of the evidence, and Bruce got in the way.

Kostas is right though, if I want to go back to the guesthouse and go through Leo's stuff, to see if there's anything to give him away, then now is the time to do it. It just doesn't sit right with me to be going further away from Sienna again, especially if Leo has got blood on his hands. I want to be around to make sure nothing happens to her. Although, we've secured the villa, and the guesthouse is only just down the road. It wouldn't take me that long to nip there and back again to have a quick rifle through Leo's possessions.

'Promise you'll keep watch on Sienna?'

'I'd give my life for that girl.' Kostas looks genuine when he says this. I have no doubts that he's a good guy.

There's no reason not to take his word. He's been by Sienna's side for years and he wants revenge on the person who took Bruce's life. He's also a trained bodyguard, so he's likely to stand a better chance of successfully stopping any threat than I am.

'You're right, I'm going. There's just something I've got to do first.'

'That's my man. I'm rooting for you. Do it for the underdog. Do it for Bruce.' Kostas gives me a wink. He pulls out a large silver keyring, jangling with a number of different-shaped keys. 'Here's the key to the guesthouse.'

Shaking his hand, I thank Kostas. Then, I stand at the bottom of the stairs and listen to the conversation on the landing above. Leaning my head against the wooden bannister, I can hear Molly's gentle voice on the next floor. Reassured someone sensible is with Sienna and that Kostas is also going to be in the villa, I turn to leave.

Before I can change my mind, I'm out the door and into the darkness. The wind has almost dropped completely but there are still spots of rain in the air. The weather is much better than an hour ago though. I check my phone, the signal is still at zero.

Heading out beyond the boundary wall, I lean against one of the palm trees briefly. I'm so close to giving into despair. Being trapped on the island, surrounded by nothing but sea, and no way to get external help is truly terrifying. I'm at my wits' end, scared for Sienna's safety but afraid for my future as well. I want to protect her, but I'm out of my depth.

I start walking again, all the time my mind turning over the last few days. Sienna's world is so different to mine but I wasn't expecting to encounter crime and murder as part of it. Perhaps the lives of the rich aren't so very different to the lives of the poor after all.

Arriving at the blue door of the guesthouse, I check to make sure no-one else is around but there isn't a soul in sight. I'm sure the majority of staff will still be in their own accommodation, waiting out the tail end of the bad weather. It's possible Hazel will be in the guesthouse, or even some staff members who might have been nearby and needed to shelter. If anyone is inside, I'll need to make up an excuse for being here but I'll cross that bridge when I come to it. Slotting the key in the lock, I pray this isn't going to come back to bite me. At least Kostas gave me a key to get in without any hassle, the last thing I need to add to my list of problems is breaking and entering.

Even so, as I step through the door and into the guesthouse, I have visions of bright flashing lights and officers in uniform. I shudder, I never want to go back to experiencing an interrogation in a sterile room or hear the clang of a jail door behind me ever again. I swore to myself that I'd get on the straight and narrow, I wanted to make something of myself and to have an honest life. I was doing so well and now everything has come crashing down around me.

I'm sure that someone is trying to frame me. The way Astrid behaved with me, the fact Leo found out about it, and the way he has been dripping poison into Sienna's ear ever since, all seems very suspicious to me.

I have to find the killer.

I have to prove my innocence.

And I have to get my wife back.

Otherwise, I could be the prime suspect for murder. And I could lose everything.

Chapter Twenty-Seven
Sienna

Someone is knocking on the bedroom door. Someone is trying to get in.

To begin with, the sound is quite low and I don't hear it over the crash of waves outside the villa. Then the knocking gets louder and more insistent. I freeze in my seat, aware there's only a thin panel of wood between me and whoever is out there.

'Stay there,' Leo instructs. He moves next to the door and barks out, 'Who is it?'

'It's only me, dear. It's Molly.'

I sit up. 'Oh, let her in,' I say to Leo. The truth is, I've been feeling more and more anxious about being shut in this room with Leo after what he said about Owen having a piece of Astrid's dress in his hand. I'm so certain that I didn't mention this detail to him and I don't think Owen would have given him this information either. My husband and I are the only people who know about Owen finding a square of the fuchsia material. Unless Leo overheard the conversation between the two of us when we were downstairs earlier? We weren't exactly being quiet, so it's plausible. But I'd rather be with Molly right now.

Leo turns to me and scowls. 'We can't just let her in. You said yourself we should remain here until the morning, until the storm has properly blown over and we've got connectivity again.'

'It's Molly,' I reply. She's practically my surrogate mother, one of the people I love most in the world. There's no reason for me not to let her in.

'Think about this,' Leo says. 'She could be out there with the killer, with a gun pressed to her head.'

'What!' I fly off the sofa, his words shaking me to the core.

'I'm not saying that she is,' he clarifies. 'I'm just saying that she could be.'

'Molly!' I call through the door. 'Is everything all right out there?'

'Yes... are you letting me in?'

'I think it's best just the two of us stay in here,' Leo says under his breath.

I'm so confused about who to keep close and who to keep at arm's length. I should interrogate Leo on how he knew about Astrid's dress, but I don't have the courage to have that conversation while I'm alone in a locked room with him. I'm feeling more and more uncomfortable about being in my bedroom with Leo, for so many reasons, so I'd rather take the risk and open up the door at this point.

I wrench the chair that's wedged under the door handle away from its current position, turn the key in the lock, and then slowly open the door a crack and peer out.

Thank goodness it's just Molly standing out there, by herself, with no gunman in sight.

Widening the gap in the doorway so she can get in, I urge Molly through. However, without speaking, she indicates with her hands that we should go downstairs. Does she know something that I don't?

I slip through the door and into the hallway before Leo can stop me.

'Sienna, where are you going?' Leo's grey eyes are bright and I can see a red flush of anger building in his cheeks.

'Molly needs me.'

'It's not safe out there, come back into the room.' His voice has a hard edge and I don't like it one bit.

'The villa has been checked over several times, it's completely secure and no-one is getting in or out without Joseph or Kostas knowing about it, they've got the surveillance cameras working again.'

'Kostas is okay?' I ask, finally feeling like there's something to be pleased about.

Molly smiles brightly, 'Yes, he's absolutely fine. We're all going to have something to eat downstairs, as it's been quite a day. Leo, are you going to join us?'

'I really don't agree with this, Sienna. We'd be much safer staying where we are. I owe it to your father to make sure no harm comes to you.'

'I'm going with Molly,' I reply firmly.

Leo isn't used to not getting his way, I watch him wrestling with his emotions before he says, 'I'll be down soon, I just need to use the bathroom.'

Molly escorts me downstairs and into the sitting room. A fire has been lit in the huge hearth and it's emitting a pleasant warmth. Instantly, I feel lighter being out of close quarters with Leo. Kostas is sitting in a squishy armchair.

'Oh Kostas!' I cry, flinging my arms around him. 'I'm so glad you're back in one piece.'

'So I am,' he says soberly. 'It's just a shame about poor old Bruce.'

The reality of Bruce's death sinks in a little bit more. It's been such an awful few hours, and I haven't been able to even begin to process my grief for the bodyguard who's watched over me day in and day out since I was a little girl.

'Let's get you some food,' Molly fusses, in her usual maternal way. 'And a drink, I'm sure you need it.'

'It's not over yet,' I sigh, trying to push down my panic that the killer is still unidentified. I allow Molly to mother me and give in to having some sustenance, even though I really don't feel very hungry.

Molly sits down beside me on the sofa and we both gaze at the fire dancing in the grate while I dive into the sandwich that she's made me.

'Good?' Molly questions.

'Very. I didn't realise how much I needed this.' I eat a little bit more and then say, 'Molly, I need your advice.'

Out of the corner of my eye, I notice Kostas discreetly rising from his chair and making his way out of the room.

'I'm all ears,' Molly says, giving me an encouraging smile.

I pour my heart out to her. 'I love Owen, I thought he was my soul mate. My gut instinct is telling me to trust him but I just don't know if I can.'

'Owen has been doing everything he can to try and protect you,' Molly assures me. 'Sometimes you have to go against what logic is telling you. You can never go wrong with following your instincts.'

I chew my lip. 'I was so appalling to him. I reacted badly this morning...'

'You were terrified, he understands that.'

'I can see now I was too hasty to blame him when he appeared on the clifftop.' I go on to tell Molly about Owen's confession about kissing Astrid the night before her body was found.

'My mind is all over the place,' I finish up, wiping a stray tear. I've cried more today than I have in months.

'He had a point though,' Molly says. 'You didn't give him a chance to explain and he did as soon as he was able to.'

'I keep focusing on the fact everyone has said I didn't know him well enough to marry him.'

'Don't listen to everyone else's opinions. You made that decision, so you must have seen something special in him.'

I remember the day of our wedding and how tender Owen was with me when we said our vows. He treated me like a princess that day and has done every day since. He's been nothing but a complete gentleman, always opening doors and making sure I have everything I need to keep me happy. Molly's right, I did see something special in Owen and I'm ashamed I was so quick to forget that.

'Is there something else that's bothering you?' Molly asks; she's always been so in tune with my moods.

'It's Leo.'

'Thought it might be.'

'He said he regrets not continuing our relationship.'

Molly's brow creases. 'Except, the two of you weren't really in a proper relationship, were you?'

Molly is of course right again. It was all very one-sided with me doing a lot of the chasing. And, after Leo went to Hong Kong, it was only a matter of months until our regular contact trickled out. He only messaged me back once in a blue moon and I stopped trying to call him, because he rarely answered. It devastated me. So I need to clear all that from my mind. I cared for Leo: a lot. But he never returned my feelings when it mattered.

I want to tell Molly about Leo's slip-up while we were upstairs together but I'm afraid about what it might mean. Could Leo really have more to do with the murders than I first thought?

'I better go and see what Joseph is up to.' Molly pats my hand and then gathers up my plate and glass. 'Let me know if there's anything else you want.'

After Molly has gone, I realise I haven't seen Owen for a while. Molly said he was doing everything he could to protect me. What did she mean by that? Is that why he hit Leo? And where is he now?

Despite all my doubts, I'm still worried about Owen. Perhaps I need to follow Molly's wisdom and go with my gut instinct. And that's telling me to stand by my husband. He's the only real thing I've ever had in my life.

I'm lost in thought when Jed comes into the room. 'Is the fire warm enough for you?' he asks.

'Fine,' I nod my head, although I'm not really in tune with the temperature of the room, I just don't want to get drawn into a conversation about it.

'Forgive me for intruding,' Jed says, hovering at my elbow. 'I have some information I think I should tell you.'

That gets my full attention straight away. 'What is it? Is it about the murders?'

'Not quite,' Jed drawls slowly.

I tense, bracing myself for what he's about to say, I get the sense this isn't going to be happy news.

'There's something you need to know about Owen Turner.'

My head spins. I've just decided to follow my heart where Owen is concerned. Is Jed going to say something to sway me from that path?

Jed pulls out his phone and presses play on a recording. I hear Owen's voice, angry and harsh, as he threatens Jed.

My hands fly to my cheeks. 'Jed, when was this?'

'This afternoon.'

'I can only apologise,' I say. 'You can be assured the matter will be dealt with.'

There's an expression on Jed's face that I don't like one bit; he doesn't seem to be upset at all, and the brittle smile he gives me makes me feel queasy.

'I appreciate it.'

'Did he hurt you?'

'Not exactly, but it was close,' Jed says. 'I will of course need to notify your father this has happened.'

Suddenly, I wonder why Jed has this exchange recorded. If Owen's violence towards him came out of the blue, then how would he have managed to capture it on his mobile phone?

'Play it for me again. From the start.'

Jed colours and I realise something is off with this. 'I don't want to listen to it again,' he stumbles. 'And there's something else.'

He's trying to distract me so I don't request for the recording to be played again, and it works.

'Owen has a criminal record.'

I try my best not to show any surprise but this news has rocked me. Owen has never mentioned anything like this to me. Swallowing, I wonder how to respond. I'm burning to know what the criminal record was for but I can't admit to Jed I had no idea. So I say nothing and my silence is rewarded with the answer.

'Owen has kept his prison sentence under wraps very well. He changed his name by deed poll, all of his papers, he's been running from his past for a long time. Until now.' Jed sniggers in a way that makes me feel unsettled. I don't think he even realises he's done it.

I'm astonished. A criminal record and a prison sentence. Owen must have done something serious.

'He's a violent man, Sienna.'

'Everyone deserves a second chance.' I don't sound convincing at all, but I have to attempt to keep my cool.

'I'm just warning you. You shouldn't trust him.'

Jed leaves me, swaggering away as though he's just told me something as unimportant as what's on the menu for dinner.

I'm reeling from the news that my husband has hidden something else from me. Jed is a member of staff, surely he has no reason to lie to me? So I'm back to where I was a few hours ago, wondering what else I don't know about the man I gave my heart to.

I glance out the window. It's still dark outside and I've got a long wait until the morning. The walls of the villa feel like they're closing in on me, and I feel weirdly claustrophobic. My slice of paradise has turned into a hellish nightmare.

I never thought there would be a time when I would want to flee this island, but now I pray for an escape.

Chapter Twenty-Eight
Owen

The guesthouse is massive, there are a number of rooms downstairs and they all look as though they belong in the pages of a glossy magazine. The villa is fairly minimalist but this property is very different, furnished with dark wood throughout and each room has its own stylised theme. There are lots of little ornaments on shelves, windowsills, and the mantel above the fireplace in the main sitting room. These, along with the wood carvings and the numerous paintings adorning walls, make the building feel more homely. Except, in the current circumstances, as I search for evidence of a killer, every set of eyes staring out of the artwork frames seem to be following me and each of the big pieces of heavy wooden furniture could be hiding a person behind them.

Scouring through the downstairs rooms, I hope I've done the right thing in leaving Sienna at the villa. I can only hope I'm the target for the murderer, and their aim is to split Sienna and me apart. This seems to make sense to me. Why else would Astrid wind up dead hours after she kissed me? I just have to hope that Sienna isn't on their hit list.

My search doesn't turn up anything, so I head upstairs and methodically go through each of the five guest rooms. The second bedroom I go into is Leo's, the scent of his aftershave hangs in the air. I yank open his wardrobe and assess his clothes but there's nothing out of place or unusual, just a row of expensive fashion labels. I throw back the sheets on his bed, not sure what I'm expecting to find, but there's nothing there. I check under the bed, in the bathroom, in his chest of drawers, but everything is organised and ordered. No items look out of place or suspicious.

I burst into the other rooms and hurriedly rummage through every drawer and scan every surface. Again, everything looks ordinary, there are no objects to cause any alarm and no sign of anything untoward. With my shoulders drooping, I'm about to slope back down the stairs, feeling deflated, when I catch sight of a final door that's slightly ajar. It's the door to the main bathroom. I enter, not expecting to find anything in here either.

At first, everything looks normal. There's a ginormous shower, complete with a waterfall shower head, which has a skylight opening above it. I've never seen a design like this before, it's incredible. I can imagine how relaxing it might be to step into a shower such as this on a blue-sky day. Currently, grey clouds roll above it, making the effect more ominous than inviting. I scan the room for a final time and, just as I'm turning to go, something snags my attention.

In the white hand basin, there's the faintest trace of a red smear. I move closer, checking it's not just my eyesight playing tricks on me, but it's definitely there. I stare down at it, as though the smudge can reveal its secrets to me. It could just be an innocent shaving cut or even blood from someone's gums. But it's the first indication I have that something is amiss, so I whirl around, looking to see if there's anything else in this spacious room that could be hiding more information. And that's when I see a thin door set into the wall just by the entrance to the bathroom. I pull it open. It's dark with no lights and I can't see anything immediately. So I feel around with my hands and, at the bottom of the cupboard, I find a wash basket. I manoeuvre the wash basket out of the cupboard and tip it on its side. Out of it comes tumbling a number of dark items of clothing. I fish the first item out and immediately drop it again in shock.

It's a balaclava.

Kostas's words come back to me instantly: he said the person who killed Bruce was wearing a balaclava and dark clothing. With a shaking hand, I go through the items: as well as the balaclava, there's a black, long-sleeved top, a pair of thick, plain tracksuit bottoms, a zip-up black jacket, dark gloves and socks. On a tropical island such as this, I can't imagine that too many people have balaclavas and thick, dark clothing in their possession. This is the evidence I was looking for.

But the discovery increases my fears Leo is behind the murder of Bruce, and likely Astrid as well. Uncovering these items could be the key to bringing the murderer to justice and ensuring that I'm not drawn into a police investigation. A wave of relief washes over me but, in just a few short seconds, a different wave of emotion rushes through my body – and this time it is one of pure terror. Because if Leo is responsible, he is at the villa with my wife and I am here.

The thought chills me to the bone. Sienna is in danger. I have to get back to the villa.

Gathering up the clothes, I go into one of the bedrooms. I prise a pillowcase off its pillow and stuff the items inside. Then, I exit the house as fast as I can. Racing to get back to the villa as quickly as my body will allow. As I'm running, there's just one thought running through my mind: *please let Sienna be okay.*

I'm so focused on my goal of getting back to Sienna that I'm not properly taking in my surroundings. I'm inches from the boundary wall of the villa when a sound rings out in the darkness. It's unmistakable. It's the sound of a gun being fired.

I throw myself against the footings of the boundary wall. I swear I just heard something whistling past me. It could well have been a bullet but it's so dark I can barely see a few paces in front of me. Frantically looking around me, I realise the fairy lights on the palm trees, near the entrance gate to the villa, must have gone out in the storm because there's no light emitting from where I think they should be. I'm in complete darkness.

Another shot booms out. My stomach clenches as a second bullet whistles past me, far too close for comfort. I need to move, I'm too exposed here, a sitting duck. And whoever has got that gun knows the rough area where I am. I lie on my front and slither, as silently as I can, away from the entrance gate. I'm guessing whoever it is will expect me to try and get back to the villa as my next move. Taking myself away from the direction of safety has every nerve in my body zinging and I'm braced for the impact of a bullet. I tell myself that at least if the person wielding the gun comes after me, I'm leading them away from Sienna.

Once I'm a little bit further along the outer edge of the wall I find a boulder and position myself behind it. I pat the ground around me as quietly as I can, and then I find what I'm looking for. There are several small rocks in the earth alongside me. So I pick up three and hurl them back towards the direction of the entrance gate. I'm not expecting to strike the gun holder, that would be too lucky. My plan is to create noise away from where I currently am, and to see if I can steer the person hunting me down into the small pool of light emitting around the entrance gate, from the lights inside.

Perhaps if I can get a proper look then I can figure out who it is and I might then be able to work out a way to fight back. After all, knowledge is power.

I hear each of the rocks clatter against the fence and fall down to the ground. I hold my breath and, sure enough, the next shot fired is towards the entrance gate. Whoever is after me has taken the bait and switched their attention further along the wall, away from where I am. I wait and I watch. Eventually, the shooter steps forward into the pool of light.

My attention is drawn to the gun first, now hanging by their side. But they're wearing a hoodie and I still can't make out their face.

I still don't know for certain who the killer is.

But I do know they're between me and the villa where Sienna is – and they have a gun.

Can I stop them from harming my wife? Can I keep myself protected?

And how many more people will die in paradise before the night is over?

Chapter Twenty-Nine
Sienna

'If I could have my time over, I'd rewind the clock and walk straight past the door to the Barker-Jones residence. Working for Derek was the worst decision I ever made. My life could have been so different.'

My mouth is agape. I'm horrified to hear an employee speak about his job and my father in this way, and even more horrified because the words are coming out of Joseph's mouth. Joseph has worked for my family since I was tiny, and I've never picked up on any indications that he wasn't happy in his role. He was the butler at my parents' London mansion and he's been working on Oyster Island for the last six years. He and Molly are more like family than staff to me so I'm shocked to hear this admission.

I left my chair by the window ten minutes ago, after becoming too agitated just sitting there, with nothing but my thoughts to occupy me. I decided to move about the house to see if I could pick up signal anywhere on my phone, without any joy. I've been wandering the downstairs rooms in the villa aimlessly until I overheard Joseph's distinctive voice. In the study, I can hear Joseph continuing to complain about his job and his life. He's in the covered porch room by the front door, where we store the flip-flops and sun hats. With both the study and porch doors open, I can pick up on everything he's saying because he's not exactly being discreet.

'The sacrifices I've made for that family over the years, working all hours of the day. And have I been properly compensated for it? Of course I haven't.' Joseph sounds more than disgruntled, he sounds angry.

'Get out while you can son,' Joseph is now saying. Before I have time to question who he's dishing this advice out to, I hear a reply.

'Thanks for the tips.'

It's Jed's voice.

I wonder how long they've been talking for and what else has been said. Perhaps I'm just very naive, but I always thought that Joseph and Molly had been so happy working for our family. And they've both been nothing but loving and kind to me my whole life. So I'm utterly dumbfounded to hear the words now coming out of Joseph's mouth.

'And Derek thinks he's being so generous, packing me off here to the middle of nowhere. It's only because he's got designs on this island himself, marked it out for his own retirement, and he wants me to be the dogsbody who gets everything perfect for him before he arrives.'

'That sounds like Derek,' Jed agrees.

'What about what Molly and I want? We had dreams of going back to Ireland. Living out our final years amongst the lush green hills and sweet-smelling air. Instead, we're still slaving away here, sweltering it is, far too hot for my Molly with her sensitive skin. Apart from tonight of course, I'm completely sodden after going out there again.'

'Why were you outside?' Jed enquires.

I hear the squelch of boots and also wonder what Joseph was doing outside again, in the torrential rain.

'I must be a fool, to keep trying to protect this family,' Joseph grumbles, avoiding the question.

I'm not sure I want to hear much more, so I sidle along the passageway, intending to slip away unnoticed, but then I catch sight of Joseph through the partially frosted glass. He's soaked to the bone with droplets of water sliding down his nose.

'How come you haven't just left then?' Jed's question floats towards me and I go still, realising I want to know the answer, curious to know what's kept Joseph here for so long.

'Molly won't leave, Sienna's like the daughter she never had. And I can't leave without Molly.'

I exhale, relieved that Molly's feelings towards me seem to be genuine, but I'm troubled by the harsh tone in Joseph's voice.

'So it looks as though I'm stuck here, in limbo. I might never taste a proper Guinness or see the streets of Dublin again at this rate.'

My heart sinks, I'm dismayed that Joseph isn't happy and I feel bad that I seem to be the root cause for his unhappiness. I'm about to turn away when it dawns on me that I could do something about this. I could organise for Joseph and Molly to have an extended holiday in their home country. If I spoke to my father about it, I'm sure I could convince him. All I have to do first is to go and address the issue with Joseph. After all, isn't it better to sort these things out rather than leaving them festering?

So I remind myself, all it takes is thirty seconds of courage to make a change, and good things can come of it.

I move towards the porch entrance and I make my presence known. Joseph instantly blanches, it's obvious he's worried that I've overheard him. Meanwhile, Jed looks shifty, his eyes are darting all over the place, looking everywhere except at me.

'Joseph, there's just something I want to say...' I'm planning to tell him how much I appreciate him and Molly. I'm also intending to offer to help them organise a trip back to Ireland, to show them how much they mean to me. But I stop in my tracks.

Because something shiny catches the light. I see Joseph is holding a silver keyring in his hand. On it is the key to the panic room.

I'm completely thrown and my words fade away. Why does Joseph have the key? Has he taken it deliberately so I can't access the panic room?

I thought I had a tight-knit circle around me on Oyster Island, but I couldn't have been more wrong. My husband, my ex, my employees, my surrogate parents, is there nobody I can trust?

Joseph looks from me to the key in his hand and back again. He sees my face aghast but he says nothing to reassure me and my stomach flips with fear as a result. Turning on my heel, I flee from the porch area. The villa is no longer a safe haven for me, so I need to form a plan to get away. Perhaps I can get down to Leo's speedboat to hide there and, when the sea has calmed, I can leave the island that way.

Looking over my shoulder, I see that neither Joseph nor Jed have attempted to follow me. My feet carry me back to the sitting room, where the fire is still burning brightly in the grate. It is chillier than most other summer evenings but it's not by any means freezing, despite the rain, so the fire feels a bit too much. The flames spit and crackle and I'm eager to get out of the stifling room.

But before I have a chance to leave, a hand sneaks out from the armchair, closing around my wrist.

I shriek.

The fingers have a firm grip on me. I try to yank myself away but fail. The figure rises up from the chair and I see it's Leo.

'It's just me,' Leo says softly, releasing my wrist.

My nerves are shredded to pieces and I just want to get out of this villa now. I'm an emotional wreck after everything that's happened today.

Leo gestures towards the L-shaped sofa, 'Let's sit for a while. You look like you need some company.'

'No, get away from me!' I shout at him.

'Take it easy.'

'How can I take it easy, when there's literally no-one I can trust in this house!'

'You can trust me.' His voice is firm.

'Leo, upstairs you mentioned Owen having a piece of Astrid's dress in his hand when we found her. There's no way you could've known that. Not unless you were watching us...'

Leo doesn't get a chance to answer. Because someone is banging at the rain-splattered window. I can see the person's fists flying, feel the window being pounded, and hear the high-pitched howls on the other side of the glass that divides us.

I bite down on my lip so hard that I draw blood. The rain is blurring the figure, their face looks stretched out of proportion, long and thin. At first I can't tell who it is. And then the wind picks up in intensity once more and I see the person's hair flying out behind them. I catch sight of the distinctive colour. It's Hazel.

Leo has a spark of recognition at the same time as me and his jaw drops in surprise.

'I thought she was back at the guesthouse!' he exclaims. 'Quick, Sienna, what's the nearest entrance to here?'

I stand motionless. I want to help Hazel but I'm terrified for my own life.

'Sienna!' Leo practically shakes me, but I shrink back from him and stand against the opposite wall. My hand reaches down to my stomach and my fingers feel the outline of the gun hidden in my waist bag for reassurance.

Leo thrusts open the big window and hauls Hazel inside. She half climbs, half falls in through the window and a cold blast of air and rain drives into the room at the same time. The fire wavers in the grate.

'Hazel, what's happened?' Leo pulls his girlfriend to her feet before slamming the window shut again. He then tries to guide her towards the seat nearest the fire, but she's frantic with panic and resists him.

'The killer is out there!' The warning note escapes from her lips, she's trembling with cold and with fear. Tears mixed with rainwater run down her cheeks, her clothes are soaked through and she has a streak of mud across her forehead.

My knees feel weak as I try to push myself back further into the wall. All day I've known that this moment was coming. It's here now. I try to talk myself into a position where I can face whatever is coming next with bravery, but my whole body feels like jelly.

'Did you hear the gunshots?' Hazel asks, her green eyes glowing with emotion.

Leo shakes his head.

'The killer was shooting in my direction. I thought... I thought...' Hazel breaks down in tears.

Leo immediately has his arms around her.

'I only just managed to get away,' Hazel pants in distress. 'I don't know how I'm not dead.'

'Did you see who it was?' Leo questions, smoothing Hazel's hair back from her face.

Hazel hesitates. 'It was dark—'

Leo makes a noise of frustration.

'It was definitely a man,' Hazel says, her breathing slowing now.

I peel myself away from the wall. If what Hazel says is true, the killer is not within the four walls of this villa. They're outside, lurking, with a gun. Or they've only just returned, my mind immediately turns to Joseph's wet clothes and whether this has any significance.

Hazel appears to notice me for the first time. She goes pale as I approach her. She hides her head in Leo's shoulder.

'It's okay, we're here to help you,' Leo says, trying to convince her that she's in a safe place now.

Hazel uncovers her face, her lip trembling. 'I think... it might be Owen.'

'No!' My voice is just a whisper. Since the moment I saw Owen clutching a piece of Astrid's dress, I've been wrestling with the question of whether my husband could be a murderer. And now Hazel is sitting here and telling me there's a gunman outside and she thinks it could be Owen. If this is true, then my whole world is about to implode.

I drop to my knees in front of Hazel. 'Are you sure?'

At that moment, the room is filled with people. Molly, Jed, Kostas and Joseph all rush into the room.

'Someone is firing shots outside,' Molly wheezes breathlessly.

'Oh my God!' I spring to my feet, the room spinning around me. What Hazel is saying must be true.

'Hazel has just been shot at,' Leo tells the others. 'We need to do something, we can't just allow the murderer to be out there on the rampage with a gun.'

'Who is it?' Joseph asks, his gaze fixed on Hazel.

'I think it might have been Owen,' she replies, her voice low and loaded with emotion.

I'm clutching at straws now, but I focus on 'might have been', still trying to hold onto the possibility that my new husband isn't a killer. I remind myself that Joseph has just come in from outside and he has taken the key to the panic room. That marks him out as a potential suspect too. But there are only so many times I can find excuses for Owen's behaviour.

'Right boys, it's time to round him up,' Kostas orders. 'I can't believe I was taken in by him.'

'You can't go out there when he's got a loaded gun!' Molly cautions.

'I can when my gun is bigger,' Kostas winks, revealing a shotgun and two handguns on the inside of his coat. 'Here you go, fellas,' he tosses the smaller weapons to Joseph and to Jed.

My heart is in my mouth as I watch old Joseph turn the device around in his hands. It's unlikely he's ever held a gun in his life. And yet, there's a gleam in his eye that I don't like. I want to snatch the weapon out of his hand, but I have to trust Kostas knows what he's doing.

'Kostas.' I move forward and clasp his hands between mine. 'Please, please be careful.'

Kostas nods. He's the only person in this room I fully trust. 'And Kostas?'

He looks at me intently, awaiting my next sentence.

'Don't shoot at Owen, I beg you. Not until we know he's definitely guilty.'

'I wouldn't take anyone's life unless I had to,' Kostas assures me. 'But if someone shoots at me, I shoot back.'

His intentions are crystal.

'Keep safe,' I say to him. And then, under my breath, I whisper, 'Keep an eye on Joseph, there's something off about him. I'm worried he might be involved.'

Kostas gives me a wink. 'Don't worry, I've got it covered.'

I watch as the three men don coats and troop out the front door, as though they are going on some sort of hunting expedition. Which they are of sorts, except my husband is the target.

I pray no-one else is about to get hurt. I just want this nightmare to end. But I've got a horrible feeling it's only just beginning...

Chapter Thirty
The Killer

Time is running out.

The storm is easing, which means help will be on the way from the mainland.

If I don't make my move soon, my chance to make things right once and for all will disappear.

While events haven't gone how I'd planned, the opportunity to fix the outcome is still within my grasp. I can still have my revenge.

And I still have one thing working to my advantage: she has no idea who I am. She doesn't suspect who is out to get her, and I intend to keep it that way, right up until the last moment. But I want her to know who I am before I kill her.

They say keep your friends close and your enemies closer.

Well I'm close, Sienna.

Closer than you know.

Chapter Thirty-One
Owen

I conjure up a picture of Sienna: her sea-blue eyes, her honey-coloured hair, her beautiful smile and flawless style. She's my everything. I cling onto a vision of her, and I let myself settle on just one of the magical moments we've had together as a couple: dancing under the stars on our wedding night. Just the two of us, uninterrupted, pressed close together and moving to the beat of the song we named ours. I hold tightly onto the image of my wife, otherwise I might just lose my mind out here.

Never in a million years did I think our honeymoon would be anything but blissful. I thought my hard times were over and I was now on a better path, with my stunning wife by my side and a whole world of opportunities about to open up to me as a result of my wife's family name. This honeymoon was meant to be the first step in our happily ever after, the beginning of a strong marriage. I can't believe how spectacularly it has all fallen apart.

My teeth are chattering with cold as a new downpour of rain gushes from the dark clouds above. I managed to successfully deflect the attention of the gun holder away from me but the reality of being so close to death has just hit me and my limbs are temporarily numb with shock. I flung a few more rocks in different directions to try and confuse them and, mercifully, the trick worked. My intention was also for the gun to lose a few more bullets and for the sound of the gunshots to alert those inside the villa to the danger outside. I just hope it worked.

Once I'm sure the path ahead of me is clear, and I've had a chance to refocus myself, I make my way cautiously towards the large entrance gate on the boundary fence. Earlier Kostas buzzed me out of the villa and my plan was to get him to authorise my return entry. When I arrive outside the gate, I see that it's wide open. I made sure to shut it earlier. Perhaps the gale has pulled the door open? But that doesn't seem possible as the wind has died down in the last half an hour. And the gate is too heavy, too big to be easily moved. Even a storm of the kind we're having isn't forceful enough to move it. So has someone else entered or left the villa?

Passing through the gate, I see three figures hastening in my direction, only paces away from me. In a matter of seconds, they come to a halt in front of me.

'Owen, is that you?' Kostas's voice rings out.

'Yes—'

Before I've finished my sentence, there's a gun pointing at my forehead.

'Woah!' My mind is racing, why's Kostas pointing a shotgun at me?

'Put your hands in the air.' His voice is hard and menacing.

I do as I'm told.

'What's that in your hand?' I see that Jed has asked the question and Joseph is standing next to him. They each have weapons in their hands as well. This makes me feel queasy. Kostas is a trained bodyguard; I doubt Jed and Joseph know what they're doing with a handgun. And that makes them far more dangerous.

'Guys, whatever's been going on, I'm on your side.'

'Answer the question,' Jed yells at me, I can see his finger resting on the trigger. He doesn't like me and he has a gun pointed straight at me. I gulp. My life really is hanging by a thread.

'It's a pillowcase containing clothes. I believe they belong to whoever murdered Bruce. There's a balaclava in there along with the dark clothing you described, Kostas.'

Kostas lowers his shotgun slightly. 'Is that the truth?'

'Honestly,' I say, trying to make my voice as sincere as possible. 'Kostas, didn't you say the murderer was shorter than you and average build? That's how you knew it wasn't me, and that still stands.'

Kostas lowers his weapon even more. I need him to accept my word. If he does, then I'm certain he will call off the other two.

'You can take a look for yourself if you like, want me to throw it to you?'

'Just place it on the ground in front of you and take four steps back,' Kostas orders.

I do as he says, trying to keep my movements as smooth and slow as I can.

Kostas takes the bag; the first thing he pulls out is the balaclava, followed by the t-shirt.

'Do you think that would fit me?' I say to Kostas, emphasising my point. 'I don't know what changed in the last half an hour to make you suspicious of me. But I swear all I want is to keep Sienna safe. There was someone out here with a gun, only minutes ago.'

'Where did you find these?' Kostas questions as he stuffs the clothes back into the pillowcase.

'At the guesthouse.'

Kostas swears. 'Put down your weapons,' he says authoritatively to Jed and Joseph.

Joseph follows his instructions immediately. But Jed is not so convinced. He still has the gun pointing directly at my torso.

'How do we know it's not you?'

'You have my word. If that isn't enough then tie my wrists, do whatever you need to, but let's not waste time, before anyone else gets hurt.'

'Jed, give me the weapon,' Kostas speaks sternly now, cautiously moving towards where Jed is standing.

Looking Jed in the eye, I realise this could be it. I think he's about to press the trigger but Kostas snatches it from his hands. The moment passes and I will be forever grateful for Kostas's interception.

The bodyguard eyeballs the waiter. 'Quit fooling around. This is why I didn't give you a loaded gun. We can get some rope on the way in if it makes you feel better but, for what it's worth, I reckon we can trust him.' Kostas casts a look in my direction.

Jed mumbles something incoherent in response.

'The three of you are out here, so who's left in the villa?' Panic-stricken, I calculate that Sienna could be on her own with Leo.

'Molly's in there,' Joseph says. 'With Sienna, Leo and Hazel.'

Not waiting to hear anything else, I set off at a run. Kostas is soon beside me and we match each other pace for pace.

'I'll go in the front door, you go in the back way,' Kostas says urgently.

I hurry round the edge of the building, checking each window as I go. As I pass the kitchen window, I see someone standing on the other side of the glass, their back towards me. Instinct makes me stop and I stand still in the shadows, watching for anything that might give me an indication of how things are unfolding in the villa.

The person half turns as they move towards the kitchen doorway, the light of the moon catching their side profile. The manic grin and flushed cheeks set off alarm bells in my mind.

Then I see the knife in their hand.

They've finally taken off their mask and shown their true colours. I can guess what's about to happen. And I've got to make it stop.

I've got to get back inside to Sienna before it's too late.

My trainers slip in the mud, slowing me down, as I skid around the edge of the pool area and run into the villa through the bar area and the games room. I have no idea what I'm about to be confronted with.

Will I get to my wife in time?

Chapter Thirty-Two
Sienna

'It wasn't meant to be like this!' Hazel screeches.

The knife is inches from me and it wouldn't take much for it to be thrust forward, and for the sharp, pointed blade to sink into my soft skin. My hands are clammy and my vision begins to blur slightly, I have to remind myself to keep breathing. It's not over yet and I have to keep in control of my senses.

Despite being subjected to threats to my life before now, this moment here is the most immediate danger I've ever been in. Other than the madwoman who tried to drag me out of the department store when I was very young, and who was very quickly stopped in her tracks, the other attempts to hurt me have all been more removed. The stalker who tried to enter my home never got past the first security alarms, the suspected bomb placed in the luggage hold of my family's private jet was found before we boarded, and various threatening letters and parcels throughout my teenage years have been dealt with by my security team.

'You should have been dead by now!' Hazel bares her teeth at me like a wild animal.

I'm stunned by the viciousness of her words. Why does she hate me so much? I never suspected Hazel had anything to do with Astrid or

Bruce's deaths. But seeing her like this now, I can believe that she's capable of anything.

Leo is on the sofa next to me, and Hazel whips her attention towards her boyfriend.

'And you had to go and spoil it all, didn't you?' Hazel snarls at him.

Leo goes as white as a sheet. Hazel darts forward and presses the tip of the blade underneath his chin.

'We could've had it all but you ruined it!'

'Hazel...' Leo whispers the name through his lips, unable to properly respond with the knife digging into his skin.

Hazel steps back and visibly shakes herself.

'Hazel,' Leo chokes out her name once more. 'Nothing is ruined, we can still be together.'

I'm desperate to look in Leo's direction to try and work out what he's playing at. But I daren't move, so I keep my focus on Hazel. Her sleek, chic look is no longer. Her silver hair is matted and tangled, after her time spent out in the storm. Much of her make-up has washed off, to reveal red, sore skin that had been hidden under layers of foundation. Her mascara has run, giving her panda eyes and making her look all the more dishevelled. Without her perfectly applied cosmetics, she looks several years older. This makes me question how well Leo really knows Hazel and how many lies Hazel has spun to be by his side.

Hazel cackles in a way that makes her sound inhuman. She's skittish and out of control, and one wrong move could push her over the edge.

'The minute you saw *her*,' Hazel spits, 'I was no longer of interest to you.'

'That's not true!' Leo protests.

I want to kick him in the leg, to make him shut up, but he keeps going. 'Sienna is my boss's daughter, that's where our connection ends. I work for the Barker-Joneses so I have a duty towards the family. And anyway, she's just got married—'

Hazel slaps Leo round the face with the hand that isn't holding onto the knife.

'That was so satisfying.' She slaps him again, harder this time.

'Oww!' Leo yelps, running his fingers over his red cheek.

Leo's admission catches me off guard. He's probably wording things in the way that he thinks Hazel wants to hear, but listening to him say that I'm nothing more to him than his boss's daughter stings me as though I've been physically slapped as well. Does he truly only see me as an extension of my father? Is that all I've ever been to him?

'Liar!' Hazel hisses at him. 'If you'd shown me some respect, instead of making a beeline for this princess the second you laid eyes on her, then things could've been different. You could've been rich too.'

Leo finally has the sense not to reply.

Hazel continues, 'I thought we had a future together, but I was so wrong about you. You only care about yourself.'

Her words are spot on and echo exactly what I was thinking. I've been guilty of responding to the attention that Leo has been showering over me in the last few days. It's been so confusing to see him behaving towards me in the way I dreamt of all the time I was in love with him. I genuinely believed he felt as though he'd made a mistake and regretted leaving me to go to Hong Kong. I thought we at least had a friendship after all the years we've spent in each other's company. But now I understand that Leo has never seen past my name and bothered to get to know the real me.

'Get out of my sight,' Hazel shouts at Leo. Her anger is palpable. Leo doesn't wait to be told twice. He's off the sofa and away from Hazel faster than I've ever seen him move.

My heart breaks a little to think that someone I cared for and trusted for so many years can leave me in this predicament to save his own neck without a moment's hesitation. Although he's been completely useless so far and has only succeeded in antagonising Hazel more, so perhaps I'm better off with Leo removed from the situation.

'So, here we are. Just me and you.' Hazel's green eyes look far too dilated. Why is she doing this? And has she taken something – drink or drugs? If she has, then the chances of me getting out of this villa alive seem all the more reduced. 'I bet you're wondering what you've done to deserve this?'

I give a small nod.

'Thought so. Someone as privileged as you would never even think that you were to blame.'

'Hazel, whatever is going on, I'm sure we can sort this out.' I don't believe my words, and she knows it.

Hazel clutches the knife in front of her again, bringing it closer to me. I shrink back into the sofa, cursing myself for not following my instincts and putting some distance between us when Leo pulled Hazel through the window earlier.

'We both know that's not true.'

Behind Hazel, I catch sight of Molly. The older woman is tiptoeing into the room, a frying pan held out in front of her. I want to yell to Molly, to get her to turn around and leave this between Hazel and me. But if I say anything I'll give her away, so I keep my mouth shut and steel myself to spring into action as she gets closer to Hazel.

'Tell me the truth then,' I say, staring Hazel in the face. 'Give me one good reason why you're doing this.'

My heart rate speeds up as Molly brings down the frying pan, intending to hit Hazel in the back of the head. But before the kitchen instrument connects, Hazel twists around and grabs the pan from Molly.

'I saw your reflection in the window,' Hazel laughs cruelly. 'Did you really think you'd take me out, old woman?'

Undeterred, Molly goes to knock the knife out of Hazel's other hand. I leap forward out of my seat, if there's two of us against one then we might stand a chance of overpowering Hazel. But she's too quick and she brings the frying pan down on Molly's head with an alarming thud.

I watch in horror as Molly falls awkwardly, landing on the rug in the centre of the room. I want to check that she's still breathing, that she hasn't hit her head too hard. But Hazel's attention is now on me again. She's blocking my escape route and I'm forced back onto the sofa.

'You know, I've got a gun in my pocket,' Hazel brags. 'I considered whether to finish you off with a clean shot but I decided this would be better.' She twirls the knife between her fingers. 'Where were we... Ah yes, you wanted to know why. Well, I don't expect that your father keeps you in the loop about everything. But he should have told you about this.'

The missed calls from my father's phone the night before the storm hit and his message to call him immediately spring to my mind. I saw them when I first woke this morning, it seems like such a long time ago now, and as it was still so early I ignored them. I was fed up with his bombardment of constant communication when I was meant to be on my honeymoon. But what if he was trying to warn me about Hazel?

I fiddle with the bracelet on my right wrist, squeezing one of the silver charms between my fingertips, trying anything I can to keep myself calm.

'This all goes back years. Leo cosying up to you was just the tip of the iceberg. It makes me sick to think that you have no actual idea about the history between our families.'

My head snaps up. This makes more sense than Hazel taking an extreme course of action due to Leo's flirtatious ways. Of course, Hazel is another person out for revenge because of something to do with my family.

'This should all have been resolved years ago. Instead, my life and my mother's life has been destroyed, all because of Derek Barker-Jones. I'm going to finish this once and for all now.'

Her motives are still unclear to me. She hasn't given away much information and I'm trying to work out what the connection is. If I had a bit more to go on, I might be able to keep her talking long enough to give me a chance to attempt an escape.

Hazel comes closer, the knife is long and sharp. In a sickening moment of clarity, I realise that she's probably planning to end my life in the same way she killed Bruce – by cutting my throat.

I'm clenching my jaw so hard that I wouldn't be surprised if I broke some of my own bones. Hazel is looming above me. This is the final split-second I have to get away, but there's pure evil in her expression and my chances of overpowering Hazel are slim. She has the knife and she's both taller and broader than me.

I now know what absolute terror feels like.

Just as I'm about to propel myself forward, with the intention of throwing my body weight at Hazel, I remember something.

I remember where I've heard the surname Fanshawe before.

Chapter Thirty-Three
Owen

Kostas and I practically collide into each other as we both reach the living room at the same time. The scene before my eyes is exactly what I was most fearful of. Sienna is within inches of losing her life. A massive carving knife is hovering too close to her slim neck and the person wielding it looks deranged.

It's Hazel.

Ever since I found the balaclava and dark items of clothing, I've had my suspicions. Part of me wanted to believe that Leo was behind this because of the burning dislike I already have for him. But Hazel was the other person staying in the guesthouse and I hadn't seen her since she pushed past me when I with Molly and Joseph earlier in the day. I assumed she had gone back to the guesthouse, to shelter from the storm. When I didn't find her there, my speculation that she could be the killer increased even more.

And then I saw her through the window of the villa, and I knew.

I throw myself towards the two women, but Kostas has a hand on my arm and pulls me back to his side. Hazel has clocked us already though.

'Owen,' Sienna breathes. I can see how scared she is and I just want to run to her, to place myself between her and Hazel.

'Go steady,' Kostas murmurs to me. 'No sudden movements, you might spook her.'

He slowly steps forward a few paces, his hands in the air. That's when I clock Molly, she's out cold on the floor. I daren't move towards her though. The atmosphere in the air is crackling with tension. I have to trust that Kostas knows what he's doing.

'Hazel,' he says in a soothing tone. 'It doesn't have to be like this.'

Hazel cackles. 'Oh yes it does.'

Sienna's eyes are as big as saucers. She's pinned to the seat, Hazel is standing over her and there's no easy way for her to manoeuvre away.

'Why are you doing this?' Kostas says, keeping himself controlled and composed. I'm sure he must have visions of Bruce lying dead on the floor of the security room, blood seeping from the fatal wound this woman inflicted. It can't be easy for him to keep his cool like this, when the person he is talking to killed his best friend.

Hazel shifts her stance to consider the bodyguard. Her head is cocked to one side. She's completely dishevelled, a far cry from the polished, aloof woman who first arrived on the island.

'You want to keep me talking, don't you? To try and give Sienna a window of hope. Well, I can guarantee you she is going to die tonight. After decades of hurt, she is going to pay. I will make sure of it.'

'Let us help you, Hazel,' Kostas says, holding Hazel's attention.

'Help me?' She laughs again, a loud and chilling sound. 'I know exactly what I'm doing. I don't need help now, I needed it twenty-four years ago. But did anyone help me then? No.'

Kostas pounces on this information. 'What happened twenty-four years ago, Hazel?' As he speaks, he inches forward ever so slowly.

I can't breathe, my fists are balled at my sides and I'm watching Hazel like a hawk. Kostas is putting his training into action but I'm gearing myself up to do whatever is needed to ensure Sienna isn't harmed.

'Sienna, would you care to share?'

My wife's lip wobbles, but she still manages to answer. 'I'm sorry,' she stutters. 'I'm not sure what you mean...'

'Of course.' Hazel thrusts her face millimetres away from Sienna's. 'I don't expect you to recall the incident that destroyed my life.'

'I was only a child,' Sienna pleads. 'Twenty-four years ago I would've been five years old, I don't understand what I could've done?'

'The shopping centre,' Hazel begins.

Sienna looks confused. 'But – you can't possibly be – that woman was much older.'

'She was my mother.' Hazel's voice is as sharp as the knife she's holding.

The dots begin to join up.

'Hang on a minute,' I say. 'The woman who tried to snatch Sienna from a department store in America when she was a little girl was your mother?'

Kostas gives me a look of alarm but the question was out of my mouth before I could stop myself.

Hazel's green eyes are glowering at me and she takes a step back from Sienna. 'Yes, she was. I never saw her alive again after that day. She was arrested and taken first to Rikers Island and then to a psychiatric prison ward at Bellevue Hospital. She died there.'

The whole room is silent, processing the details Hazel has just shared.

'If it wasn't for her,' Hazel jabs her finger towards Sienna. 'My mother would still be alive right now. Instead, the last time I saw her she was stretched out in her coffin and she looked nothing like my mother.'

Sienna gasps, silent tears rolling down her face. 'I had no idea. I'm so sorry.'

'I was ten years old when she was taken from me and fourteen when she died. I had no other family; she was the only person I had. So I spent the rest of my childhood going from foster home to care and back again. You can't begin to imagine what that was like.'

'No I can't,' Sienna agrees. 'You went through so much.'

Hazel looks startled, as though she wasn't expecting such a sincere reaction from Sienna.

'Nothing can make up for the loss of your mother or the things you experienced as a child. But if there's anything, anything I can do—'

'Now, this is what I was expecting. For you to beg, for you to chuck your money at me. But, like you just said, nothing can make up for my loss. No amount in the world can change what happened. I know this is what she would've wanted, a life for a life.'

Hazel lunges at Sienna. The knife is still in her hand.

'Stop!' Kostas shouts, his large hand wrapping around Hazel's arm. 'Your mother wouldn't have wanted you to go to prison, to endure what she endured. She would want you to live your life for her.'

'How the hell do you know?' Hazel spits, kicking Kostas where it hurts. He loses his grip and doubles over for a beat.

'Because my father went to prison, he died there too. I get it...' Kostas keeps talking, somehow not losing his focus even though he's in pain. 'But I didn't go running around killing people in revenge, I made something of myself instead.'

Hazel tosses her silver hair. 'It's too late for me now, I'm two bodies deep already. If things had gone to plan, the other two needn't have died. I only wanted her. That would've been enough. And then of course, my path to wealth would've opened up.'

'What do you mean?' I can't stop myself from asking again, Hazel's story is full of complexities and contradictions.

'With Sienna out of the way, who do you think might've inherited Derek Barker-Jones' wealth?'

I shrug, unsure where this is going.

'Not you, that's for sure!' Hazel mocks me. 'It would be Leo of course. Derek trusts him completely and, without an heir, he would be the natural successor to Derek's empire. His business protégé. I'm sure Leo would take full advantage as well.'

It's apparent to me that Hazel is completely deluded. She's created an imaginary future that plays to her desires.

'How does that sound to you?' Hazel turns her gaze to the back of the room. Leo is lurking there, I hadn't even realised he was here.

'I had it all planned out. Leo and I would be married and then of course Derek would have a little accident. The money, the power, the fame, everything that *she* has,' Hazel points towards Sienna once more, 'would be mine.'

I'm astounded by Hazel's admissions and I can see that Sienna and Kostas are too.

'Can I ask you something?' Sienna asks timidly.

'Go ahead, it'll be the last thing you do.'

'Why did your mother try to abduct me?'

There's a collective intake of breath as everyone in the room waits for the response.

'She was your father's lover,' Hazel says matter-of-factly.

'She was what?' Sienna repeats.

'Your father and my mother had an affair. He treated her badly. Cut her out of his life, despite being aware of how much she loved him. He wouldn't reply to her, he froze all communication. Took what he wanted and then left her high and dry after he promised her everything. It was the only way she could get his attention.'

'So she tried to steal a child?'

'That's enough!' Hazel's mood suddenly switches from reflective to angry. In a flash, she springs forward, straddling Sienna and yanking her head back.

'No!'

Kostas is only a nanosecond behind, he hooks his arm around Hazel's neck and drags her off Sienna.

'Sienna!' I lift her out of the chair and carry her to the back of the room, placing her on her feet beside Leo, who is looking shell-shocked.

Holding her close for a second, I draw back from her. There's no time to lose and, even though I'm not comfortable leaving the woman I love with Leo, he's the only option I have right now. 'Look after her this time,' I bark at him.

Swivelling back to where Hazel and Kostas are grappling on the floor, I think the bodyguard has got Hazel under control. But she still has the knife in her hand and, as I approach, she slashes it against Kostas's arm, causing him to cry out in pain and loosen his grip on her.

Hazel takes the opportunity and disentangles herself from Kostas. She springs up on her feet, her whole being focused on getting back in front of Sienna.

So I block her, placing myself in her path. Whatever doubts Sienna has had about me, I'm ready to put my life on the line to save my wife.

Chapter Thirty-Four
Sienna

Everything appears to be happening in slow motion. I watch horror-stricken as Hazel slices Kostas's forearm and rolls away from his clutches. When she stands up, Hazel's green eyes lock with mine and she comes hurtling towards me.

Instinctively, I put my hands up in front of my face to try and shield myself. Leo is standing uselessly by my side. But before Hazel can get to me with the knife, Owen's frame comes between the two of us. My husband has stepped in, without hesitation, to protect me.

I sob involuntarily as I see Owen trying to knock the knife out of Hazel's hand. I press my fingers to my lips to stifle my distress. Owen doesn't succeed and Hazel's hand remains clamped tight around the wooden handle. The determined expression on her face tells me she's not letting go of her weapon without a fight.

The truth of who Hazel is and why she's really here has rocked me to the core. I still have nightmares about the mousy-haired woman who grabbed my small hand in her sweaty one and tried to extract me from the world I know. I dread to think what she had in store for me and no amount of therapy has been able to remove that fear completely.

I try to step forward, to assist Owen, but Leo holds me back. I realise I'm shaking so I stop resisting him and my arms go limp at my sides. I knew there was something about Hazel that was familiar, but with all that make-up and her fancy clothes, she managed to hide her resemblance to her mother very well. If we had spent more time together, perhaps the shade of green of her eyes might have been more of a warning sign or I might've remembered the significance of her surname. Somewhere in the recesses of my jumbled memories is the knowledge that my would-be abductor had a child who bore a different last name to her – the name Fanshawe.

Owen managed to catch Hazel's arm again and, this time, he knocks the knife clean from her hand. My heart leaps, perhaps finally this is all coming to an end. Hazel swivels around but Owen grabs one of her wrists tightly and is intent on enclosing the other. I dig my nails into the palms of my hands and pray this is now over.

Discovering the woman's connection to my father has been mind-blowing. I was only five years old at the time and my recollections are of what happened in the department store. My initial panic when I realised the green-eyed woman was a stranger is the emotion I experience over and over again in my nightmares. I recall the noise of the store alarm, the security team that came swooping down on us, and the feeling of being back in the warm, safe arms of my nanny. Everything that came after that is a complete blur. Snippets of my parents' conversations after the event are lodged in my mind but in no particular order and I was never aware the woman was my father's spurned lover. Perhaps if my father had shared his secret and reinforced the name of Fanshawe to me, things would be different right now.

Kostas recovers and advances towards Hazel and Owen. My heart leaps for a second time, as surely this has to be the end of Hazel's attempted revenge. But, all of a sudden, the tide turns. Hazel bites down hard on my husband's arm and his grip is momentarily loosened. She takes advantage of this and frees herself. Diving to the floor, her hand outstretched for the knife. Kostas does the same but Hazel is too quick.

In a sickening flash of movement, Hazel is standing tall once more and she thrusts the knife into Owen's side.

'No!' I scream.

Owen staggers and lands on the sofa at an awkward angle. Kostas hasn't dropped his focus and jerks Hazel away from Owen. And that's when I see her reach into her pocket.

'Kostas, she has a gun!' I yell.

Hazel is distracted, her eyes gleaming in delight at the sight of my husband bleeding. Kostas kicks her feet out from under her and pulls both her arms behind her back. I wriggle free from Leo and join Kostas. Being so close to Hazel makes my skin crawl, but I force myself to be in such close proximity so I can remove the gun from her pocket. It's better to disarm Hazel than to fumble under my clothing to try to unzip the weapon in my waist bag. Breathing heavily, I point it at Hazel.

'Sienna,' Kostas says, a warning tone in his voice. 'She's not worth pulling the trigger for.'

Hazel stills and seems to understand her defeat, the fight goes out of her. At the same time, the room suddenly becomes busier. Joseph hurtles in and crouches down by Molly's side. I'm thankful to hear the older woman cry out and, out of the corner of my eye, I see her turn onto her side, at least she's not still out cold. Jed also moves into the room with some rope and helps Kostas to secure Hazel's wrists. Two other staff members appear too, their faces wear frightened expressions but they conduct themselves with composed manners. One of them rushes to help Molly and Joseph.

Satisfied Hazel is properly detained, I pass the gun to Kostas and cross the room to Owen. Dropping down by his side, I see he has lost a lot of blood and the knife is still sticking out of his side.

'Oh Owen.' I hold his face in my hands and kiss him on the forehead. A faint smile plays across his lips. 'I'm so sorry,' I tell him.

Owen shakes his head ever so slightly. 'It's okay.'

'I should never have doubted you.' He has proven his love for me and paid the price. Guilt mixed with anxiety churns in my stomach.

'I love you, Sienna,' he says softly.

'I love you too.'

I bend my face to his, my tears falling uncontrollably now.

I'm terrified that Owen is going to die.

Chapter Thirty-Five
Owen

Sienna is with me and she's safe. And that's all that matters.

I keep holding onto this thought as she kisses me and the pain sears through me. I wince, I need this damn knife out of me. I try to move my arm to assess the damage but my shoulder feels as though it's frozen. A hot shot of pain bursts down my side as I try to move and I cry out.

'Hey buddy, we've got you,' Kostas says, crouching down beside me. There's someone else beside him, perhaps another member of staff, I'm not sure as my vision is beginning to blur.

Kostas moves me so that I'm lying on the floor but, despite how gentle he's trying to be, I'm in agony. A number of faces are swimming over me now. One of them is Leo's and I can't help but think – was he involved in Hazel's plan? How much did he really know? Or did Hazel dupe him as well?

Kostas is talking to me as he presses something against my mangled side. I assume he's trying to stem the flow of blood but my whole torso now feels like it's on fire. There's a lot of activity going on around me and I'm frustrated that I can't keep focused on what's going on. Hazel is still a threat as far as I'm concerned.

'Jed has got communication up and running now and we've got word to the mainland,' Kostas is telling me. 'A helicopter is on its way; we'll have you sorted in no time. Don't you worry.'

Then I hear Molly and I'm instantly soothed; she has that effect on people. Alcohol is gently tipped into my mouth, and I pray it helps to numb the pain that's ramping up inside me.

'Owen, stay strong. We've got the rest of our lives ahead of us,' Sienna is whispering to me.

Having Sienna back with me gives me all the incentive I need to fight for my life. From the instant we met I loved her. No matter what people might think, my feelings and intentions towards her are honest. I've never felt about anyone the way I feel about her. Until the other couple arrived on their holiday everything was perfect. I have to cling onto that. I understand why Sienna was afraid and why she mistrusted me. Hopefully now she'll see how much she means to me.

I struggle to keep my eyes open but a fresh wave of pain washes over me.

And the world goes black.

Chapter Thirty-Six
Sienna

'Please stay with me, Owen,' I sob.

My husband has just passed out and I'm afraid he won't wake up again. I hold his hand in mine, willing him to be okay. I can't believe our honeymoon has ended up like this, with a blade buried in Owen's side. And it's all my fault.

I let other people's opinions and cynicism about our marriage and Owen's motives for being with me take over my own thoughts. Despite the loving way Owen looks at me, despite how we are when we're together, curled up just the two of us, and the beautiful things he says to me, I allowed doubt to creep in.

The last twenty-four hours have been a rollercoaster, but the one person I should've trusted was Owen. He was trying to protect me but I pushed him away. Leo's persuasive words about why Owen wasn't good enough for me, why he thought the 'gardener', as he referred to him, could be behind the two deaths, confused my own feelings, preyed on my anxieties and turned me away from the man I married.

I realise now the fright I felt when I stood on those sandy clifftop steps was because I'd just found a dead body and because of the mantra my father had instilled in me: trust no-one. If Owen hadn't found me so quickly, then it's likely I wouldn't have directed any of that initial fear towards him. It's too late to change anything now, and it's too late to undo the damage caused by Hazel. But the thought of Owen dying, as a result of my behaviour, is too much to bear.

I can hear a commotion going on behind me. Several of the men are with Hazel, she's kicking and screaming now, demanding to be let go. My temper flares within me and I want to go and direct it all towards Hazel, to scream back at her and to make her see how much devastation she's caused. I feel sorry for the way she lost her own mother but that doesn't excuse her actions. Astrid and Bruce didn't need to die. Hazel didn't care about the futures she was cutting short, the families left behind or the fear they both must've experienced in their final breaths. I want to make her pay for everything she's done.

'Keep talking to him.' Molly is by my side and she wraps an arm around me, bringing my thoughts back to Owen.

'Molly, are you all right?' I take her in, she looks flustered but otherwise she seems to have come out the other side of her encounter with Hazel relatively unscathed.

'A bit sore, but lucky it wasn't any worse.'

We both stare down at Owen as she says this. His chest is rising and falling in regular breaths, but he looks deathly pale.

I do as Molly suggests and I talk to my husband. I recount one of our day trips when we were staying in Cuba. I took Owen to Havana, as he'd never been before. We took a trip in one of the old-fashioned American cars and spent the evening strolling hand in hand as we walked underneath the plant-filled balconies in the historical part of the city. It was bliss. I'd do anything to be back there with my Owen right now.

I'm pulled out of my memories by a surge in voices. Diego is now here too, attempting to help escort Hazel from the room. She bites down hard on his arm and he lets out a number of expletives in Spanish. But she doesn't wriggle free this time, because Kostas and Jed also have a firm grip on her. Eventually, they manage to manoeuvre her out the door, and out of my sight.

Owen groans in pain.

'Will he survive?' I whisper to Molly.

She hugs me a bit tighter. 'He's taken a bad blow but he's a young, strong man and he's still breathing and where there's still life, there's still hope.'

I nod at this, I've got to be brave. I can't go to pieces now, I have to do everything I can to help Owen recover.

'As I said, keep talking to him, your voice will do wonders.'

So I do. I cover him up with a blanket that Molly passes to me and I talk to him in a low voice. I repeat my love for him over and over. And I keep talking about the memories we've created so far and the ones still waiting for us to make.

I just hope it's enough.

And I cross my fingers that medical help will be here soon. We're on an isolated island and, even though the storm has now dropped, the weather still isn't the best. It could take a while for a helicopter to reach us.

The longer we wait, the less chance Owen has of surviving.

Chapter Thirty-Seven
The Killer
Hazel

If I hated her before, I hate her even more now.

I'm furious that Sienna Barker-Jones got away from me. And I'm even more furious that I ended up getting caught. This is not how I planned things to be. At all.

I just hope that her husband dies. Then she'll know what it's like to lose someone she loves. Just like I did.

The one small comfort I have is that I know I'm not the only person out to get Sienna. She and her family have plenty of enemies. And it's only a matter of time before someone succeeds in bringing them down.

And when they do, I'll be celebrating...

Chapter Thirty-Eight
Sienna
Three months later

Standing on the balcony of my bedroom, the sunlight plays on my face and the sight of the sea in the distance soothes my heavy heart. I never thought I'd want to return to Oyster Island after everything that happened. Travelling on the boat from Cuba with my father, following our long plane journey, I almost requested for us to turn around. But now I'm here, I'm glad I've come back.

Hazel transformed paradise into a living nightmare but, as difficult as it might be, I don't want to give her the satisfaction of tainting this beautiful island. I want to reclaim Oyster Island as my favourite place in the world and banish away the horrible events of a few months ago. I'm going to have to work through a lot of issues in order to truly feel happy here again but I want to face what I experienced and build a future for myself on the island.

A new life for me and a new life for Owen. After a tense few weeks, my husband finally pulled through the danger period and he's now slowly recovering from the injury that Hazel inflicted on him. I've been by his side night and day. I wouldn't wish the pain he's endured on anyone, but going through this has ultimately made us closer and stronger as a couple.

Tonight, we're having dinner together for the first time since before Owen was in hospital. It will be a liquid meal for him, but it's the first step towards normality and I'm so relieved that his recovery has been as good as can be expected. He was extremely lucky because the knife didn't go in too far or hit any major organs. He hasn't suffered any infections since and he's kept himself positive throughout the whole process. The way he's handled everything has deepened my love for him. Nothing could come between us now.

Tearing myself away from the exquisite view, I give myself a once-over in the mirror before going downstairs. My face looks more drawn than it used to and my eyes are tired from all the sleepless nights I've had in the last few months: tossing and turning as I wondered if my husband was going to pull through, and more recently filled with apprehension for Hazel's upcoming trial. I fix my flower headband and give my cheeks another sweep of blusher and then I make my way downstairs.

'You look dazzling,' Owen tells me. He's waiting at the foot of the stairs for me in his wheelchair.

'Likewise,' I respond. And it's true. Despite the trauma his body has been through, Owen still looks utterly handsome and his brown eyes have retained their playful twinkle. He's had the most terrible time but he hasn't lost his sense of humour or harboured any blame for the blow he received.

Owen takes my hands in his and kisses them.

'Are you feeling okay, being back here?' I check. I wasn't at all sure about us both returning when Owen first suggested the idea, but he didn't seem fazed at all and wanted to finish off our honeymoon properly.

'Never better,' he smiles up at me.

'I'm so sorry, Owen—'

'Sshh,' he says, pressing a finger to my lips. Every time I try to apologise for my part in the events that led to him being stabbed, he won't hear anything of it. He tells me it's all in the past and he just wants to move forward with our married lives.

He's forgiven me completely, which just goes to show what a good person he is. Another man may have walked away from my crazy family. Or another man might have been angrier about my interactions with Leo and decided that I wasn't worth the hassle. But he didn't do either of those things. He's stayed with me and he has kept telling me that he loves me every day since. And I wholeheartedly believe him. There's no doubt in my mind now that Owen and I belong together.

I wheel Owen towards the terrace, where a table has been made up for four. A place for me and Owen and a place for my mother and father. They've accompanied us on this trip so we can spend time together and my parents can get to know Owen better. And we're also going to discuss plans for Oyster Island. I'm still keen to maintain the magic of the island so I still want to have a say in my father's proposed changes. But, in the past few months, I've come to realise that change is inevitable and necessary. People and places can't stay the same forever, we have to move on and move forward.

Owen glides to his spot and I settle in my seat. We hold hands across the table and I look into the eyes of the man I married. Owen confessed something to me after he came out of the private hospital. He told me about his troubled childhood. At eighteen his mother, the only parent he and his sister had, died suddenly from a short illness. He was left to help his fifteen-year-old sister navigate her tricky teenage years, acting as a parent figure to her until she turned eighteen and went to university. He sacrificed his own education and prospects, taking whatever jobs he could to make ends meet. At twenty-one, with his newfound freedom, he went wild on nights out. One of those nights turned sour and a stranger started to beat up his best friend. Owen jumped into the fray to help and he caused some damage to the person who'd hurt his friend. He had to spend a short stint in jail as a consequence, although his sentence was short because he confessed and because he was defending someone. He was out in half the time due to good behaviour. But his desire to become a gardener and make something of himself was the one positive result of the whole sorry episode. And, for that, I'm grateful otherwise we might never have met. Owen's protective streak also makes more sense to me now as well, given everything he had to do for his sister. We've promised each other no more secrets.

It's been a tough ride so far, and the media have been non-stop in their intrusion. The headlines have kept on coming, rife with speculation, and Hazel's trial is going to be a complete media circus. Both Owen and I will have to give evidence. Once that's done, she should be out of our lives. There's enough evidence against her for Bruce's murder and she's also confessed to killing Astrid as well. I don't see why we have to go through the farce of a trial when Hazel has already said she's guilty, but it's the law.

'Daddy!' I jump up and kiss my father on both cheeks. My mother follows him and I greet her in the same way.

'Good evening,' Derek says. 'A perfect night for us to dine together.'

My father and mother both take their places. My father is wearing a white cotton shirt and chinos, he has a gold chain at his neck and a sovereign ring on his little finger. It's the most low-key I've ever seen him dress. My mother has blow-dried her hair and she's wearing a floaty, pastel dress. She's seated next to Owen.

'How are you doing?' she asks him.

'I'm fine thanks,' Owen assures her politely, even though I know he's continuing to experience pain and still having to take a cocktail of medication each day. 'I've had a good rest today after the journey and I'm looking forward to tasting Molly's cooking again.'

As he finishes his sentence, the woman herself appears, as if summoned.

'Ah, how lovely to see you all together,' Molly beams with delight.

'And you Molly,' I say warmly. Molly and Joseph are going to be here for the next month while we settle in and then they're going off on their own adventure to Ireland. I'm so pleased for them. I found out the reason Joseph took the key to the panic room was because he wanted to be ready to usher me safely in there if needed. He was trying to help me. Unfortunately, that didn't work out because none of us thought Hazel was the threat and Joseph wasn't able to react quickly enough. My father heard about how Molly tried to fight off Hazel single-handedly with a frying pan and he rewarded them handsomely for her efforts to save me. I mentioned Joseph's wish to spend some time in his homeland and my father got his personal assistant to arrange the whole trip for them. They've both been beaming ever since.

'I've got soup coming up for you,' Molly tells Owen, who is still on a liquid diet.

'Music to my ears,' he grinned. 'I've missed your cooking.'

Molly flushes with pleasure. 'And risotto for the rest of you.'

We all thank her and she scurries back to the kitchen.

'Well, a toast is in order,' my father declares, popping the cork to a bottle of champagne. He fills up each of our glasses.

'Can you have some of this?' my mother checks.

'I'm sure a sip or two won't hurt,' Owen winks.

'To family,' Derek begins. 'To my darling daughter and her brave husband. I can never thank you enough for protecting Sienna. So most of all, to Owen!'

We all clink glasses. 'To Owen!' I echo enthusiastically.

Owen has gone crimson, which is something I've not witnessed before. But rather than being unsettled by this, it fills me with happiness. Because my husband is here, he's alive, and we've got the rest of our lives to keep discovering new things about each other.

After a turbulent start to our marriage, I hope this is an end to all the drama now. I hope this is truly the start of our happily ever after. But I have a horrible feeling that's just wishful thinking and there's still more trouble to come...

Chapter Thirty-Nine
Owen

Derek Barker-Jones hands me a Cuban cigar and pats me on the back. 'I don't make a habit of saying thank you but, in this case, it was essential. And I'm going to say it one more time: thank you for saving my daughter.'

Derek's about-turn in the way he interacts with me has taken some getting used to. I'm relieved he has finally accepted me as his daughter's life partner but it's just a shame it took me getting stabbed for it to happen.

'Your marriage has my blessing now, son,' Derek tells me. 'In fact, I think we should have a proper wedding celebration for you both. Mark the occasion in the style it deserves.'

'I'm not sure how Sienna will feel about that... She wanted to avoid the big white wedding and what she wants, I want.'

Derek strokes his jaw. 'A wise man. You've worked out how to keep your wife happy quicker than I did.' He takes a swig of his rum.

He's had a few drinks by this point in the evening and it's loosened his tongue. He's less reserved, less calculating in his speech. Sienna and her mother have gone to have a chat with Molly in the kitchen and the two of us are still sitting on the terrace, underneath the inky night sky.

His words make me remember Hazel's claim that her mother had an affair with Derek. I wonder if it's true, or if it will become a focus of the trial. I'm done with secrets so I ask him outright.

'Did you really have an affair with Hazel's mother?'

Derek looks at me sternly. 'No, I never met her mother. She was a stalker. Completely besotted with me and would go to any length to get my attention, including trying to abduct Sienna.' But he doesn't look at me as he's saying this, and I'm not sure I believe this is the whole story.

He takes another sip of his drink and coughs. 'I should've kept tabs on her daughter. I should've known that something like this might happen...'

'You could never have predicted this,' I try to reassure him.

'It was shoddy of me. I knew the daughter had a different name from the mother, but in the mists of time I'd forgotten it. Perhaps if I'd kept her name with the security team all this would never have happened.'

'You can't change the past,' I shrug.

'That's right, young man, I can't. But I'll always be grateful for the part you played in protecting Sienna. So name your reward. Anything you want, it's yours.'

It's not at all surprising that Derek has said this, he's one of the world's wealthiest men so I know he literally does mean anything I want. There is one thing I want, but it's something money can't buy.

Taking the first puff of my cigar, I lean back in my wheelchair. 'There is something.'

'Name it.'

'Sack Leo Harrison.'

'Sack Leo?' He looks confused. 'Why? He's my best employee.'

'I don't trust him.'

Derek scrutinises me and then says, 'Because he was with Hazel? She's already told everyone that Leo wasn't involved. He had no idea who she really was or what she was planning.'

'And you believe Hazel's word?' I challenge.

'No, but I believe Leo's. I've had the discussion with him already, of course I have. But that boy's like family to me, I've known him since he was a fresh, green teenager. He's not a threat.'

'That's what I want,' I insist, not willing to back down on this. Everyone else may be taken in by Leo, but I'm certainly not.

Derek frowns. 'I just said no. Leo is my most trusted employee, I'd lose a lot of money if I let him go. And he's heavily involved in my retirement plans.'

This is what I was worried about. Derek won't hear a bad word said about Leo and, more than anything, I want him out of Sienna's life. If he's to feature in the future plans of the Barker-Jones empire, then we're going to have to keep seeing him. And I'm not sure that I can stand that.

'Okay,' I say, choosing my battle. 'I don't pretend to understand the rules of business. If you won't get rid of him, then would you at least pull him off the development project for Oyster Island and let Sienna run it with my help instead?'

Derek bites his lip. It's a familiar action, the same thing Sienna does when she's deep in thought. 'Sure, if it means that much to you. It would be good to see Sienna getting involved in the business. But the two of you better show me that you can handle it.'

'I promise you we can.' I hold out my hand and we shake on the agreement.

We carry on drinking and my mood lifts. Perhaps I can build a positive relationship with my father-in-law and find some common ground with him. We start out talking about the island and possible landscaping of different areas. The conversation is pleasant and ordinary. Just what I need after everything that's happened.

But Derek keeps knocking the drink back. I can't keep up with him, his alcohol tolerance is way higher than mine and I shouldn't really be drinking much because of the medication I'm on. So I make sure to slow down, not wanting to put a foot wrong now he's finally accepted me and not wishing to impact my recovery.

'So what happens with Hazel?' I ask Derek. 'Will she go down for double murder?'

Derek shifts uncomfortably in his seat.

'She will. I'll make sure of it.'

'I guess it's not good publicity for you?' I didn't mean to voice this out loud, but I couldn't seem to stop myself. The story has been splashed across newspapers and media sites since the day after Hazel was arrested.

'No, it's not,' Derek admits. 'I was intending to make the island into an exclusive resort, somewhere people pay big money to spend time. So two dead bodies are the last thing I needed.'

He pours himself another rum, but I wave him away when he tries to refill my tumbler.

'It doesn't matter though, there's always another news story. It just means we will have to delay the plans a little.'

'More time to get things ready then, I suppose.'

'Exactly.'

Derek is slurring his words now and his eyes look a little glassy.

'Do you think there's enough evidence to convict Hazel?'

'There is. There're enough witnesses too. I'll make sure justice is done for Bruce, he was a loyal employee. And I'll make sure that poor girl's family are compensated too.'

I wasn't expecting Derek to look so cut up about the death of two of his staff but perhaps I'm being too hasty to judge the man.

'I feel responsible for Astrid's death,' he goes on.

'Responsible?' I sit up a bit straighter, my senses zinging. Why would Derek feel responsible when he wasn't even here?

'She was here because of me.'

'Astrid? Your recruiters hired her, surely?'

'I hired her.' Derek's words are clipped. 'I hired her because she looked like Sienna.'

'Why?' I'm a bit baffled by the direction this conversation is heading in.

'As a decoy.'

'You knew something was going to happen on the island?'

'Of course not,' Derek replies abruptly. 'It was a test.'

I open my mouth but no words come out. I have no idea what he means.

'I employed Astrid for the purpose of trying to seduce you. To try and break up your marriage to my daughter.'

I go to stand up in surprise but pain lances through my side and I fall back into the wheelchair, almost overturning the table in the process. I watch some alcohol slosh out of one of the glass tumblers. There's a rushing sound in my ears and I grit my teeth until the pain subsides.

I'm boiling mad and trying to make sense of what Derek is telling me. How can this be true?

He lays a hand on my arm. 'I did it to try and protect my daughter.'

'Protect her?' I say incredulously. 'You almost scared her out of her mind!'

Derek juts out his chin. 'Sienna's made of tough stuff.'

Does he seriously believe this? After all Sienna has been through in her past. Would he really put her through something like this just to get rid of me?

It crosses my mind that Derek might just be messing with me right now, but who would joke about something like this?

'Jed helped to orchestrate everything. I was setting you challenges. Why do you think you got so drunk on the first night Leo and Hazel arrived – Jed was giving you double measures.'

He's serious then. Now I get why Jed was going out of his way to be hostile and to antagonise me. It was on Derek's orders.

'You passed the test. You won.' Derek gives me a dark smile. 'We've shaken hands. End of.'

I'm flabbergasted. How can he expect me to be okay with what he did?

'What about Sienna? Are you going to tell her?'

Derek shrugs. 'I don't see why she needs to be told. I didn't know there would be a real threat on the island as well, otherwise I would never have done it. But it's my island and I can do what I want here. I thought you should know though.'

I'm shocked. Derek is passing this off so breezily, unable to see the harm he's caused. He's the puppet master and is more than happy to pull other people's strings to suit his purpose. A chill runs through my core.

'Was Hazel anything to do with you?' I have to ask this question.

Derek looks thunderously at me. 'I can assure you Hazel was not part of the plan. As far as I knew, Leo was just bringing his new girlfriend. I sent him to the island on purpose, to throw another distraction into your honeymoon. But I would never intentionally have put Sienna in any real danger. End of discussion.'

I exhale. It's going to take me a while to process what Derek has just told me. Maybe if I tell Sienna she will properly forgive me for kissing Astrid. She says she has already, but the information I was set up would help to dispel any remaining uncertainty she might have. Or maybe her father's twisted actions will screw her up even more...

I reach out for the cigar. Derek's reveal has sent me into freefall but he's behaving as though it's no big deal. As if it's an everyday occurrence for your father-in-law to organise a honeytrap to try and destroy your marriage.

Half an hour ago, I thought Derek and I might stand a chance of building a bond between us. Now I realise he's every bit as unhinged as Hazel, more so perhaps. He has the money, power and resources at his fingertips to do whatever the hell he likes. There's nothing to stop him.

I take a drag on the cigar and try to calm my shredded nerves. Derek is now talking about football fixtures, how quickly he's moved on. I haven't and I won't forget what he's done.

Now, more than ever, it's clear that Sienna needs me – someone to help her navigate her crazy life and to look after her.

We both sit there, puffing on our cigars, and I consider the future. My father-in-law is clever and calculating. So I'm going to need to be on my guard and to learn to outsmart him. Derek may think I'm satisfied with Leo being sidelined away from the island renovations but that's not the case.

Leo failed Sienna multiple times when her life was in danger and he's made his hatred for me more than apparent. So I'm not about to let any of this go.

I'm going to protect Sienna from Derek Barker-Jones and Leo Harrison and their self-serving ways. And if that means finding a way to remove either of them, so be it.

Chapter Forty
Sienna

I can't believe what I've just heard my father tell Owen... or perhaps I can. I'm stunned to discover my father hired Astrid specifically to try and break up my marriage. And it very nearly worked. Of all the things my father has done to exert his control over my life, this is the very worst. Astrid is dead as a result of his twisted actions. My father may not have killed her directly, but he was responsible for her working on Oyster Island and for her being near the clifftop on the night she died. He is by no means free from guilt.

That wasn't the only troubling part of the exchange between my father and my husband. My father's voice shook as he answered Owen's questions about Hazel's mother. By now, I can't believe a word that man says. It's possible he really did have a liaison with Hazel's mother. Which would make everything that followed his fault – the attempted abduction, Hazel's mother's prison sentence and death, and Hazel's quest for revenge.

I turn to leave from my hiding spot by a large, old palm tree but my stomach drops when I see someone has been standing inches from me. I'm not the only person who's been eavesdropping. Just a few paces behind me is my mother.

'I heard every word,' she confirms icily. 'And don't think I'm surprised.' She indicates for me to follow her into the villa.

'Sit,' she commands as we enter the kitchen. I perch myself on a high-top chair at the island worktop, knowing better than to push back when my mother has such a thunderous look on her face.

I take her in as she opens her handbag. She's movie-star beautiful with her perfectly blow-dried hair, glamourous cobalt blue dress and long limbs. But her shoulders are tense and her mouth down-turned. I've seen her smiling less and less in recent years. I shiver as I wonder how she is going to respond to my father's admissions.

'Here,' she passes a thick, cream envelope to me. 'Open it.'

'I slide my finger along the back of the envelope and carefully unpeel it. I manage not to rip the paper in the process. Next, I ease out the contents inside. My hand is shaking slightly.

'Read it,' my mother instructs, although her voice has softened a little.

I scan the words printed on the letter and gasp. 'Is this true?'

My mother nods grimly.

'Hazel is my half-sister?' My voice comes out in an uncertain squeak.

'She's your older half-sister,' my mother confirms.

'So... she wasn't lying.'

My mother exhales. 'No, she was being truthful and so was Deborah, Hazel's mother. At the time, your father kept the details of her claim well away from me – and the media. I suppose it was easier to cover affairs and flings up back then, there was no social media for starters. I've done my own digging though and I now know some of what happened.'

I reach over and put one hand on top of my mother's. My head is spinning with all this information, but I can see my mother needs me to be strong right now. I straighten up, and steel myself to face whatever revelations come next. If there's anything I've learned in the last few months, it's that your inner strength is your most important asset.

'Deborah and your father seem to have dated for almost a year, it wasn't even a one-night stand. It was so much more than that so no wonder the woman was infatuated. I found a source who has said Deborah believed Derek was going to propose to her. This was several years before he and I met. But Derek had been stringing the poor woman along the whole time. Their interactions were conducted in secret, he told her it had to be that way because of his profile. He left her devastated. It seems she found out she was pregnant a few months after he dumped her but he didn't believe the baby was his. He put the poor woman through hell, she seemed to be going through a legal process to get him to take a paternity test but she didn't have the money for the kind of lawyers Derek had. His legal team ran rings around her while she was trying to raise his first-born. That's when she snapped and came up with the plan to grab you and demand ransom money.

'Oh my god...' A flashback of the moment the tall, dishevelled woman tightly clasped my hand comes back to me. The fierce look on her face, the fire in her eyes. It all makes sense now.

'He thinks he can do whatever he likes and get away with it,' I say out loud, without really meaning to.

My mother nods in agreement. 'It's been that way for too long. No-one has stood up to him – including me – it's time for it all to stop.

'What do you mean?' I ask her.

'This has got to stop,' she repeats. Her eyes are glassy and she blinks away tears. 'This is just one of the many selfish choices your father has made which has destroyed someone else's life.'

I know she's right. I just wish it wasn't true.

'The other affairs he's had...' she gazes out of the window lost in though for a few moments before continuing. 'The business decisions where he's prioritised money over all else. The people he's crushed on his way to the top in both his personal and professional life. And the loss of life he's set in motion, all because he desires to be in control and for everything to go his way. And now two people are dead... and he almost got you killed too. It has to end, before any more people get hurt.'

She turns to look at me, and sweeps a stray hair from my face, tucking it behind my ear. She twists a strand of the honey-blonde between her fingers, it's the same colour as her own hair. 'We've always been so similar me and you. We've let him get away with too much. It's time for us to be strong now.'

My mother gives me a quick hug and then she leaves without another word. I wanted to ask her how she's planning to stop my father, but I was afraid of what her answer might be.

Wandering back out to the terrace, I hope to find Owen. But he and my father are no longer there. They're empty glasses are all that remain. I try to steady my racing thoughts by focusing on the beautiful sandy beach and the expansive sea. As I do, I spot my mother winding down the hill – and my father is with her. I see her pass him a glass of something, and then they disappear out of sight.

I think I know where they're going and, in a few more minutes, my hunch is proven right. They're walking hand in hand on the beach. My mother used to tell me stories of when she first came to Oyster Island, when my father proposed to her here and had the villa built for her as a wedding gift. Why did everything go so wrong for them? Was it the money, the power, the fame?

My father is weaving all over the place, he looks more than tipsy. My mother, in contrast, is straight-backed, her posture is perfect. I want to run after them, to slip in between them and tell my father to change, to make him listen. I'm rooted to the spot, I know it's far too late for that.

They walk out towards the sea, their figures getting smaller. They look just like a normal couple on holiday. The sky is darkening and it gets harder and harder to focus on them. But I keep standing here anyway, lost in my thoughts, and wondering how everything got so messed up.

Epilogue
Sienna

My bare feet sink into the white sand as I make my way across the beach to the sea. I stand at the water's edge, placing my toes into the warm froth and I watch the gentle lapping of the waves around my ankles. The last few months have been the worst of my life, but it feels like the nightmare is finally over. My father is gone. His bloated body washed up on shore two days after he took a drunken walk along the beach. A part of me will always be grieving for him, always wondering how things might've been if he'd behaved in a different way or taken an alternative approach to life. But he'd destroyed too many lives. I don't condone what my mother did and I don't think I'll ever come to terms with it. But she's free now. Free to live her own life, and already she's putting her vow to live a better life into action and using her money to set up more charitable endeavours. At heart she is a good person but, like Deborah, she got overwhelmed by my father's web of lies and acted out of character. She was pushed to her limit by an egotistical man who had been lying to her for most of their marriage.

Despite everything Hazel did, I can't help but feel bad for my half-sister. She was just an innocent child when she was parted from her mother. If fate had twisted another way, I could very well have found myself in a similar position to my older sister. Could I have coped in that situation? Would I have reacted in the same way? I don't honestly know, but I do know Hazel could've had a better life if my father had been a better man. I've arranged to fund her mental health support, it's the only thing I was permitted to do. It's perhaps too little, too late but I felt I had to do something for her as my father had neglected his responsibilities to her.

My mother has been charmed by Owen and they're getting on so well with each other. I feel like I have a real family unit now. My mother is less distant these days and, although we're bound together by her secret, I know she was motivated by love for me and she wanted me to have a future that was determined by me, and nobody else.

And I am looking to the future now. I place one hand on my stomach, gently cradling the new life within. I suspected my pregnancy only days before we returned to Oyster Island with my parents. I'd been feeling nauseous and tired, but I'd put this down to the traumatic events Hazel set into motion and the anxiety I felt around Owen's recovery. My doctor confirmed I'd just reached the three-month mark, which means this child was a honeymoon conception. This has given me hope because, even though so much damage was done on that holiday, this child is the silver lining to that dark time. Owen was over the moon and I can see the news has given him a new sense of purpose, a new reason to heal. We had a scan a few days ago and seeing the tiny human wriggling inside me was the most wonderful moment. I hope this baby will represent a new start for us all and help to strengthen the relationship between my husband and mother.

The only black cloud hanging over us is the resentment Owen still feels towards Leo for bringing Hazel to the island. Even though Leo has protested he had no knowledge of who she was, Owen can't forgive him. My father had already taken Leo off the project to rejuvenate Oyster Island before he died and, as I'm standing here, Leo is currently winding down the Hong Kong office. I feel sorry for him as, since my father died, his plans have been unravelling as fast as mine are coming together. I wish we could've remained friends. After all, he was a big part of my life and I believed him when he said he didn't realise Hazel's connection to my would-be kidnapper from all those years ago. But not everything can work out in the way we want. Now my father's businesses are being torn down and sold off, I can't concern myself with Leo. I'm sure he'll land on his feet somehow. I have to keep the distance between Leo and Owen, it's best they don't cross paths again. I'm sure Leo will thrive whatever he ends up doing next and I wish him well in his new chapter. There are no hard feelings on my part but Leo is my past and Owen is my future. I should never have doubted that.

Now, my focus is going to be on my husband, our new baby and creating a life together on this beautiful island.

I'm going to make sure everything is just perfect.

Epilogue
Leo

I'm off the hook... for now.

Derek the old fool didn't fire me. I thought my job, my reputation, my lifestyle was over after Hazel – my girlfriend – attacked Sienna. She was the apple of her father's eye, the most precious thing to him, so I was sure that my life as I knew it was over.

But I was given a second chance. Derek trusted me like no-one else, I made myself valuable to him. The plan was for me to gradually take over the running of the Barker-Jones empire as he retired. He regarded me as the son he never had. And I was more than happy to step into his shoes. But then he had to go and ruin it all by getting himself killed. I have my suspicions as to how his accident in the sea really played out. And that's something I will be pursuing in the future.

At the moment, I've got my work cut out. Iris Barker-Jones is hell-bent on destroying everything Derek built up, with no regard to the financial losses. I guess when you have the amount of money they do, a few hundred thousand here and there is spare change. That suits me though, because I'm taking advantage of the scatter-gun and un-professional way Iris is handling everything. Sienna really doesn't have a clue about how any of the business operations work, which has very much worked to my advantage. I've been able to cream off significant sums of money without either of them paying any attention. More importantly, everything is in chaos. Contracts that were relying on the Barker-Jones empire to deliver are panicking, big projects are close to finishing but they're without guidance. And that's where I step in. I'm making the most of this opportunity, it could work out better for me than me taking over the reins from Derek. Because now I can do things my way and the world really is my oyster, I've made sure of that. There's just one thing that's out of my reach... Sienna.

Even now, I'm still kicking myself for not keeping in Sienna's good books while I was working in Hong Kong the first time. I was so focused on supercharging my career that I thought she would wait. How very wrong I was.

I'm still shocked Hazel killed Bruce and Astrid, and that she was after Sienna. I really didn't suspect her at all. I thought she was just a social climber, with me for whatever materialistic gains she could make. As it turned out, her intentions were far more sinister. If I'd been aware that she had plans to hurt Sienna then of course I wouldn't have taken her anywhere near her, let alone to a secluded island. I know Sienna herself was suspicious of me when I slipped up and mentioned Owen having a piece of Astrid's dress when he came upon the body. But the only reason I knew that was because he had the brightly coloured material in his hand when he was trying to bash down the door to the guesthouse. Sienna forgets, in that moment, she was scared of her husband. Thankfully, Hazel confessed everything, and told everyone I had nothing to do with Astrid or Bruce's death. If she hadn't, then things would have been much more difficult for me.

I'm surprised Owen Turner hasn't come after me. Then again, he's still recovering from his injury. I'm going to be keeping a close eye on him and Sienna from now on. I'm certain their marriage isn't going to last, they're from two different worlds, he doesn't deserve her. It's a shame Hazel didn't finish him off, as it would've left my path to Sienna clear.

But I've had setbacks before and I'm not about to let what happened on Oyster Island or a man like Owen Turner stand in my way. I'm determined to have everything – the power, the money, the perfect wife – so my quest to win Sienna back doesn't stop here. I was so close to breaking up their marriage and Hazel had to ruin everything. So I'll watch and wait until the next time Owen messes up. And, if that doesn't happen, I'm sure I can find another way of making her mine...

Extract
The Christmas Party

Prologue

Now

I spin with my sister in the middle of the dance floor, our hands
clasped tight, whirling round to the music just as we did when we were
children. The DJ is playing yet another classic Christmas tune and we
both shout along at the tops of our voices, smiles wide, eyes bright,
mirroring each other. Rainbow-coloured disco lights shine across the
vast room and the crowd around us shimmers and sparkles.

The moment I've been hoping for is finally here. After ten long years, my family are together under the same roof again. My two sisters, my mother, our children and our husbands. We're reunited after a decade of not speaking. But I don't want to think about the terrible night that shattered our family because I've waited for this day for a long time.

As the song ends, I stagger, wobbling on my high heels and putting a hand to my throbbing head. I feel a steadying arm loop through mine and I'm guided along the edges of the friends and family gathered here to celebrate in this exquisite hotel. The hotel that my wealthy husband and I own. We've spent the last five years remodelling the place and I've poured everything into making this building a beautiful home as well as a successful business. I've worked hard to be where I am today. I may have had a little help with my husband's money and contacts but I came from nothing. So tonight I'm proud to show off amongst my nearest and dearest. And I know I've earned every single one of the admiring looks that have come my way this evening.

Everyone else seems to be in the moment, lapping up the festive atmosphere, but I'm on edge and I can't seem to properly let my hair down, despite the champagne that's flowing. A huge Christmas tree dominates one corner of the room, while the warm gold and red colour scheme spills out across the rest of the space and throughout the multitude of plush rooms beyond. Everything looks perfect on the surface. But, right now, I need to get away from the party.

When I exit through the double doors, the noise instantly dims and I feel like I can breathe properly again. I make my way along a winding corridor, my sister's hand in mine, and then we swing open another set of double doors into the grand foyer. This is the dazzling focal point of the building, with its curved marble staircase and sweeping gallery complete with a glittering crystal chandelier.

The first thing I notice is the strange silence. The sounds of the party in the background shut out by the soundproofing.

The second thing I notice is the dead body. Lying spread-eagled on the white marble floor, a pool of dark red blood surrounding the head like a halo.

I'm stunned, surely this can't be happening? But my sister inhales sharply next to me so I know I'm not imagining this.

This is not a horrible dream. It's real.

My heart is hammering in my chest and my mouth feels dry. I lift my chin and make myself look once more at the person lying on the floor. I immediately recognise the broken figure at the foot of the steep marble staircase.

And I scream...

The Christmas Party is available to order now!

Extract
The Christmas Holiday

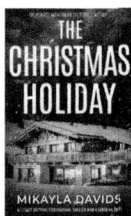

Prologue

Now

I trudge through the snow, my breath coming out in puffs, visible in front of me in the frosty air. I scan the hazy horizon, I can barely see anything past the end of my own outstretched hand.

My feet sink into the clean snow. There are no other footprints, no one else has been here for some time. So where is everybody? How have I managed to get so lost?

I keep walking, slow heavy steps, my boots are dragging me down and my body aches with the effort it takes to keep going. I can't stop, I need to get back to the lodge, otherwise I'll freeze to death out here.

The snow is coming down hard now and, just as I start to despair, I see a light in the distance. It must be the holiday lodge where I'm staying with my family. It has to be.

I stumble forward, eager to get inside, to find warmth. But then I see something in the snow, just ahead of me. Something still and unmoving on the ground. But it's unmistakeable.

A body.

Spread out like a snow angel, hair fanning out across the white, soft blanket beneath it. A trickle of bright red blood from mouth to cheek, frozen in a moment of time. It looks unnatural, someone has positioned the person in exactly this way to make a statement.

That's when I hear the sirens. The blue flashing lights come closer. And then the German shepherd Garda dogs rush towards me, followed by the shouts of men in uniform.

They speed closer, the gap between us narrowing by the second. I'm clearly the target, but, any minute now, they're also going to spot the lifeless shape on the ground in front of me.

They will find me.

And they will find the dead body.

The Christmas Holiday is available to order now!

Dear reader,

Thank you for choosing to read *The Couple on Holiday*. This is my third psychological thriller and I absolutely loved writing this story. It was wonderful to lose myself in creating the setting of Oyster Island, especially as I was writing this book in the depths of winter. The joys of fictional escapes! I also had so much fun planning the twists in the story! If you were entertained and would like to find out about my new releases, you can sign up to my mailing list via the following link: https://subscribepage.io/MikaylaDavidsBooks

Subscribe!

I hope you were gripped by *The Couple on Holiday*! If you were, I'd be so grateful if you could post your review on Amazon. Reviews on Amazon make such a huge difference, especially for newer authors like me, and they help other readers to discover new stories.

Leave a review!

It has been my lifelong goal to write books and – after a lot of dreaming, sleepless nights and many hours at my laptop – it's finally happening! I've poured my creativity into this novel and I'd really love to hear your feedback now the characters are out in the world. Did you fall for Owen? Who were you suspicious of? Would you spend your holiday on Oyster Island?

If you would like to get in touch with me, you can do so via my Facebook page, through Twitter or Goodreads.

All my thanks,

Mikayla Davids

Follow me on Twitter: @MikaylaDBooks

Follow me on Instagram: mikayladavidsbooks

Find me on Facebook: Mikayla Davids Books

Visit my website:

https://mikayladavids.wixsite.com/mikayladavidsbooks

Acknowledgments

It's a wrap! My third psychological thriller novel is written! I loved the time I spent escaping to Oyster Island, so I hope you did too. My first thanks goes to you, the reader. None of this is possible without your engagement, so whether you've discovered this story on Kindle Unlimited, in paperback or via an ebook download, I thank you for taking the time to read my words. It really does mean so much. (Please let your friends and family know if you'd recommend – or better still, pass the book along!)

I've been absolutely blown away by the response to my first two novels – *The Christmas Party* and *The Christmas Holiday*. So if you've been following my writing journey and you've read these books as well, another massive thank you from me.

If you haven't, what are you waiting for?! You can dive into the Bailey sisters' family reunion in *The Christmas Party*. Which of the three sisters will you love and which will you love to hate? And you can discover whether or not Alicia survives her first Christmas holiday in Ireland with her new husband and her in-laws in *The Christmas Holiday*.

I've dedicated this book to my husband because he is very much my partner-in-crime in writing. He helps me to storyboard my ideas, he's been my first reader on each book, pointing out spelling errors (hello Russel in the bushes!) and encouraging me to keep going when my hand is sore from typing! He's also been working hard behind the scenes to publish the novel. There are so many things we're both still learning about self-publishing. And I'm so glad that we're working on this as a team.

Thank you to my children, who inspire me to keep striving every day. Sometimes following your dreams turns out to be hard work! But I want to be a role model to you both, so that you can see that anything is possible, as long as you believe and persevere.

I also want to thank my parents and my in-laws for helping to entertain the children while I'm tapping away at my laptop. And thanks to all of my friends and family who've been so supportive and for your cheerleading each step of the way. Special mentions to Angela, Nicola, Charlotte, Rachel and Kim. Thanks to my writing pals, M and K, for Tuesday night troubleshooting! And to The Alchemists for being a source of writing support for the last decade.

Rhian, thank you for your copyediting magic! It's a pleasure working with you and I'm so grateful to have your input.

Thank you to The Unicorn Barbell Club and Coach Kellie (https ://www.coachkellie.co.uk), who is such an inspiration and helping to keep my body moving while my brain is plotting!

My final thanks is to Kelly Lacey of Love Books Tours (https://k ellylacey.com/love-books-tours) who has been so supportive (I highly recommend to other authors) as well as the wonderful bloggers who have given their time to read and review this book.

Also By Mikayla Davids

The Couple on Holiday: A completely addictive and gripping psychological thriller with a heart-stopping twist

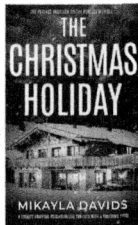

The Christmas Holiday: A totally unputdownable psychological thriller with a shocking twist

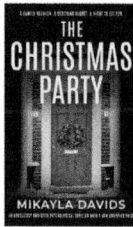

The Christmas Party: An absolutely addictive psychological thriller with a jaw dropping twist *(The Bailey Sisters Book 1)*

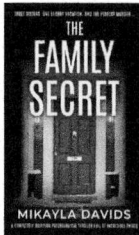

The Family Secret: A completely gripping psychological thriller full of incredible twists *(The Bailey Sisters Book 2)*

ISBN: 978-1-7392278-7-6

eBook ISBN: 978-1-7392278-6-9